Dedalus Euro
General Editor.

Mother Pleiades

Another Pleiades

William Heinesen

Mother Pleiades

(A Story from the Dawn of Time)

Translated by W. Glyn Jones

Dedalus

Dedalus would like to thank The Danish Arts Council's Committee for Literature and Arts Council England, London for their assistance in producing this book.

Published in the UK by Dedalus Limited,
24-26, St Judith's Lane, Sawtry, Cambs, PE28 5XE
email: info@ dedalusbooks.com
www.dedalusbooks.com

ISBN 978 1 907650 07 9

Dedalus is distributed in the USA & Canada by SCB Distributors,
15608 South New Century Drive, Gardena, CA 90248
email: info@scbdistributors.com   web: www.scbdistributors.com

Dedalus is distributed in Australia by Peribo Pty Ltd.
58, Beaumont Road, Mount Kuring-gai, N.S.W. 2080
email: info@peribo.com.au

First published by Dedalus in 2011

Printed in Finland by Bookwell
Typeset by Marie Lane

The Author

William Heinesen (1900-1991) was born in Tórshavn in the Faroe Islands, the son of a Danish mother and Faroese father, and was equally at home in both languages. Although he spent most of his life in the Faroe Islands he chose to write in Danish as he felt it offered him greater inventive freedom. Although internationally known as a poet and a novelist he made his living as an artist. His paintings range from large-scale murals in public buildings, through oil to pen sketches, caricatures and collages.

It is Dedalus's intention to make all of William Heinesen's novels available in new translations by W. Glyn Jones. Published so far are: *The Black Cauldron, The Lost Musicians, Windswept Dawn, The Good Hope* and *Mother Pleiades.*

William Heinesen is generally considered to be one of the greatest, if not the greatest, Scandinavian novelist of the twentieth century.

The Translator

W. Glyn Jones read Modern Languages at Pembroke College Cambridge, with Danish as his principal language, before doing his doctoral thesis at Cambridge. He taught at various universities in England and Scandinavia before becoming Professor of Scandinavian Studies at Newcastle and then at the University of East Anglia. He also spent two years as Professor of Scandinavian Literature in the Faeroese Academy. On his retirement from teaching he was created a Knight of the Royal Danish Order of the Dannebrog.

He has written widely on Danish, Faeroese and Finland-Swedish literature including studies of Johannes Jorgensen, Tove Jansson and William Heinesen.

He is the author of *Denmark: A Modern History* and co-author with his wife, Kirsten Gade, of *Colloquial Danish* and the *Blue Guide* to Denmark.

His translations from Danish include *My Fairy-Tale Life* by Hans Christian Andersen, *Seneca* by Villy Sorensen and for Dedalus *The Black Cauldron*, *The Lost Musicians*, *Windswept Dawn*, *The Good Hope* and *Mother Pleiades* by William Heinesen.

He is currently translating *The Tower at the Edge of the World* by William Heinesen.

I

A CANDLE IS LIT

The Beginning

In the beginning was neither heaven nor earth nor things, but only a vast longing for warmth, food and sleep. Life came to you like shower upon shower; tempests of tenderness filled your primal darkness, teeming rivers of milk and cleansing water, ceaseless springs of good and earnest sounds that had not yet become words. And in time, your eyes developed their first soul, and you saw the dark outline of the great giver of life, the source of all things, the one who creates and sustains, Her who is Eternal.

Indeed, before you were yet able to sense the sun and the day, a light was lit within you when you first beheld human eyes, the eyes of the eternal One.

In the beginning, you aren't this person or that, and you don't live here or there. You rest in your mother's arms and are but a nameless son of the earth. And together you two are but a link in the endless procession of mothers and children awaiting whatever dispensations fate has in store for them.

Rapacious and idle powers lie in wait for you, patient and innocent as the two of you are. The emissaries of death seek you out to lead you away from the joyous morning light of the ages into the shadowed valleys of fear and distrust that know no peace. Monsters with hard mouths and witless eyes devoid of pupils seek to determine your lives and your fates and grind you to meat in their querns. It may be that obscene fetishes will enslave you and defile your dignity, the greatest dignity life possesses, that of the mother and child.

Or perhaps, child, you will be granted a happy lot in security and peace, who knows? Perhaps you have been born to happiness, boy. Perhaps your life will go smoothly and quietly in happy and active obscurity. Or perhaps you will become a hero and liberator, a benefactor of mankind.

But perhaps you are to be counted among those who, in the finest flowering of youth, are to be sacrificed on a battleground for the sake of a simple hunger for profit, under an old murderous general with chauvinist eyes behind his leather mask. Or perhaps you yourself will become one who hates and destroys, or a hypocritical sermoniser or a revolting, treacherous flatterer and lickspittle.

Or perhaps your life will only be a poor, flickering candle that soon burns down in its holder or is blown out while the newly-lighted flame is still blue and weak.

But for the moment, you are simply *there*, and yours is a warm and damp primeval world, from the mists of which things are just beginning to unwind and take shape, slowly and hesitantly. Time encloses you in vast swaddling clothes; you will live for countless ages before your nature finally crystallises into a personality. Only then will your time start moving. But slowly, slowly, with years as long as centuries.

But seen from outside, it is all but a brief moment, only a shooting star in the night.

Only a Small Town Story

Aye, for of course it's only Antonia, the daughter of the little grocer called Jacob Sif, who has given birth to a son. And this little event should not be a reason either for triumph or for hanging your head or embarking on prophecies about the end of the world or its redemption.

Mrs Ida Nillegaard, the midwife, has performed her duty once more and with a surly expression has given a loyal and firm hand to sinful life, ably supported by Trine the Eyes and Urania Mireta, and these three sibyls are now sitting over a cup of coffee after a good day's work. Not the usual coffee substitute, but real, murderously strong and coal-black coffee from the little supply that Jacob Sif has kept in reserve since that unfortunate year 1914. Along with this rare beverage, they are partaking of freshly baked sponge cake, which Trine the Eyes, who keeps house for Jacob Sif, has managed to make for the occasion. The golden cake is so exuberantly saturated with the strength and sweetness of egg yolks that it *whispers* when you touch it. Three candles are giving off their light on the table, not spluttering substitute candles, but simply pure wax candles from those blessed days before the war.

Mother and child are sleeping peacefully, and from the open bedroom door there comes the scent of soapy water, clean linen and tarred jute. Ah, here is star-twinkling peace and blissful rest. A child has been born, and so that thing has happened again that shall happen until the end of time.

The sibyls are enjoying this moment, though not in peace and elevated silence as would have befitted these chosen to assist fate; no, there is no end to their chatter. Trine's eyes flash in competition with Mrs Nillegaard's pince-nez, and Urania Mireta, hard of hearing as she is, opens her mouth and eyes wide and extends her long neck in order to hear better. She zealously absorbs the words' rich seeds, allowing them to germinate in her virginal mind and produce warm flowers, tempting and terrible. For these three elderly women are perambulating in this world's exuberant garden of sin and shame. Exploring the tree of life and knowledge, whose untended, dark foliage tickles their necks and runs up and down their spines and awakens their horror, their spellbound disgust and their need to find an outlet in righteous indignation and intense prayer.

It is not Antonia's little early history on which they dwell, her unfortunate engagement to the honest teacher Napoleon and her outrageous affair with the dissolute and thieving lout Peter the Gravedigger. No, this subject is put aside for the evening and is only of secondary interest. For what concerns people now, here as elsewhere, is the *Eggertsen scandal*.

Eggertsen, the preacher and vacuum cleaner salesman, the great orator and Anabaptist, whose ranting could terrify, but whose forgiveness was so gentle. Eggertsen, who could soften hardened hearts in both rich and poor. Aye, for of course it was through Eggertsen that the wealthy merchant Ammon Olsen and his entire family had joined the Anabaptists. Eggertsen with the bushy eyebrows and the silvery temples and the singing voice and the unfailingly kind and artless look, who could nevertheless rage and threaten, clean up and destroy. Eggertsen, the driving force behind the great collection on behalf of the new meeting house, the "Vineyard".

The inconceivable has happened in that this man

Eggertsen has suddenly disappeared, going off first to England and then to some unknown place. He has disappeared from baptismal tank and congregation, from vacuum cleaner and Vineyard and from the committee responsible for making collections; and at the same time, Chamisso's pretty daughter, Jutta, has disappeared as well. Vanished along with Jutta Chamisso and Eggertsen are twenty thousand kroner, which this dishonourable, sanctimonious vacuum agent has appropriated from the building committee.

And after Eggertsen's disappearance, such a lot more has emerged that can't stand the light of day, things which people can only whisper or talk about with their eyes down or screwed up. And rumour still spawns new examples of the power the Devil exerts over Eggertsen's heart and over so many other human hearts, especially those of women and girls. And one story leads to another and more join them, and the shuffling dance of whispers and rumour winds its way through the steep streets of the little town and in and out of the huts and houses, shops and workshops, boarding houses, abstinence societies and illicit bars. And church-goers, sportsfolk, chess players and other respectable people who have never fallen under the influence of Eggertsen rub their hands, and the Seventh Day Adventists headed by the old bank manager Ankersen suddenly find they have wind in their sails, for what else is a man like Eggertsen but the prophet of the Anti-Christ, heralding the approach of the Whore of Babylon and the end of the world.

Trine's eyes flash zealously.

"And what punishment," she says, "what *punishment* awaits Eggertsen, if not here, then at least in the beyond."

"Yes, *punishment*, yes, indeed," repeats Urania Mireta plunged into dreams of horror.

"Yes, but ... oh no!" Mrs Nillegaard shakes her head. "Even so, as good Christians we mustn't hope ...!"

But with merciless eyes, Trine unlocks the ancient snake pits of revenge and retribution, in which eternal darkness resounds with tears and the gnashing of teeth.

But now, for a while, we will completely ignore all this fuss and cheerfully return to the beginning of time.

Dithyrambic Conditions

In the beginning, before night and day or winter and summer had yet emerged in the world, everywhere was ruled by ungovernable sorrow and unlimited joy, and the sorrow was linked to loneliness and the joy to being together with the One, that Great One.

You awaken in your wet swaddling clothes and fill the room with the perdition-fearing cries of some drowning creature; your cup of despair is full; you are enveloped by loneliness; the Void seeks you and seeks to undo all that has been done and to return you to lifeless planets. The Moon and ice-cold Mars seek your presence, the insane planet Jupiter is out to smother you in its amorphous eiderdowns of horror – you can sense its poisonous vapours in the reek of ammonia.

But all of a sudden you are surrounded by earthly kindness; you feel its good waters around you, its corn and nuts and healthy salts flow with the milk into your mouth and turn into the unstoppable growth force in your blood; its animal innocence and the soft peace of its plants come to you in fresh clean shawls, and the human eyes of the Blessed One shine on the resurrected world like two stars.

This primeval drama is repeated and renewed several times a day, as has happened for millennia. Loneliness is ever as fateful, and ever as surprising and joyful is the aversion of doom. Ah, Mother Earth, you who are perhaps the only haven of happiness in the entire universe! Ah, you who are eternally young, the only living thing among frozen and charred corpses, among skeletons and mummies and terrifying chimeras! You, who of all the planets are blessed by the Sun; you the fresh fruit of hope; you who radiate sweetness and strength in the midst of your pitiful lame and blind and retarded sisters!

Antonia, the young mother, spends her days and nights in her own enchanted world, an island in time, a happy moon, inaccessible to all except Him, the boy, the rebirth of life and the ultimate meaning. Up above her head shine sun and stars, far beneath the soles of her feet there opens a turbulent chasm of vanished days and nights. Down there are the regions she frequented until quite recently – a strange thought, a melancholy thought, indeed really quite absurd.

The past has not really gone away. It is simply just hidden for the moment beneath a radiant veil of joy, an aurora borealis of lonely ecstasy. Seen through this joyous veil, everyday things and figures fade like grotesque caricatures. Accusatory voices, bleakly conjuring, fill her ears, but this, too, feels unreal; the words disengage from each other and lose their meaning; the poison ebbs out of them and becomes diluted in the fresh morning breeze of jubilation. Sin and sorrow, shame and punishment and repentance – for each of these knives she has a sheath of smiling indulgence, and nothing can penetrate the armour of her happiness.

How fair you are, Antonia, in the infinite purity and vitality of your joy. You rest supreme in your new dignity as a mother. You know your power and know that without your breath and sighs the air would be but a cheerless trifle, and without the gracious smile of your eyes, there would be neither sun nor moon, and all the stars shining in the heavens would languish eternally and lose their power and darken to a void. "Oh, you're my doll, my secret room, my dust in the sunshine, my tabernacle, my philosophy, my eraser, my most sacred candelabrum." So sings the happy mother as she lifts up her freshly washed and newly wrapped child to the winter's sunset sky.

She reigns supreme and can say whatever she wants; her freedom of speech is unbounded, her torrent of words flows happily out into the universe. Never shall it meet resistance, be censored, be the subject of comment or made into the object of psychologists' hesitant analysis.

"You my archbishop, the prize I was lucky to win, my heavenly home, my toothless trinket, my cabin boy, my Genghis Khan, my pair of scissors."

She kisses the little face, which grimaces devotedly and uncritically beneath her ecstatic importuning. From her exquisite linguistic ability it is clear that she has gone through school and knows her geometric formulae:

"You are my loveliest tangent, you are my square, you are the hypotenuse that's the sum of the squares on all the right-angled sides! You are my Lucidarius, my old book of knowledge, my Copernicus and Newton! Yes, you are my Isaac Newton, my beloved Isaac Newton, for I've always loved Newton and will always love both Kepler and Newton as well as Galileo. Oh, you, my Leaning Tower of Pisa, if only you need never collapse and go through the realm of death and rise again and sing your song to the lamb and the throne."

Here, it can also be seen that she has kept up with religion. But, as she puts the confused child to her breast, she continues:

"Ah, you my press, my wine press, my tear press. Then press, my Persian press, drink of the white juice of the press, drink of the Persian sea. Yes, turn and twist your way through life with those tiny hands that are like sweet-smelling rosebuds, like love-struck lettuce and sprouts, or like Michelangelo Buonarroti! You, you, my Buonarroti, my angel of life, you crazy thing, you gift from Moses and Pharaoh and Potifar's wife and the heavenly king Jesus Christ! You chirrup, up, up."

She recalls Brorson's wonderful hymn, which comes to her aid in her search for words; she sings it at the same time as she half eats the little virtually hairless head and moves it over to the other breast:

> Oh, my Sulamith, yes mine, yes mine
> All I possess is also thine

She closes her eyes, almost incomprehensibly rejoicing in life and distorting her young face in a sob betokening bliss. And here, her knowledge of literature and world history again comes to her aid:

"I tell you, you are my personal physician to the King of Macedonia, you are my prince from Asia Minor, my advertisement column, my Sultan of Eritrea, my publican and sinner and postmaster general called Godskesen-Hansen! You shall be called Alpha and Omega, the beginning and the end, you shall be called Ariel and the Ancient of Days and the sum of the angles."

He has had his fill now, and the milk seeps generously and superfluously from the corner of his mouth. He smells of water and soap, of milk and honey and towel, of manna and wild grapes; he gives a protracted sigh from the effect of boundless abundance, and their eyes meet in oceanic satisfaction.

Now he wants to sleep. Now he wants to wander into eternity again, to that little spot among the celestial bodies where he has his Bethlehem, to the Pleiades, the celestial curtained bed of all small children.

"And sleep in safety, you my little alabaster flower, you my brochure, you millionth part."

She kisses him once more and overwhelms him; she sheds tears of happiness, and in ecstatic high spirits and pain she sings a hymn that she herself makes up on the spur of the moment:

> And from sufferings of the world
> There came a rose so red and fresh
> A rose there came from in my flesh
> A lily from my knee unfurled.
> There came a rose from my left breast
> A rose there came from my right breast.
> A lily rose all red and white
> The poor world's sufferings to requite.

II

MANIFOLD LOVE

Magic Lantern

Jacob C.F. Hansen Grocer is the inscription in sea green lettering on the sign above the door of Jacob Sif's little shop. The name *Sif*, which sounds so piquant and makes one think of strange ancient Egyptian deities, is only a nickname formed of course by combining the two letters C and F.

Jacob Sif's shop is both crowded and old-fashioned, but there is a special compelling, cosy feel to it that other shops, whether large or small, cannot really live up to even if they do their very best. It has a soul of its own, whatever it is this soul consists of.

Perhaps it has to do with the fact that it is always filled with the sound of whistling and humming, snatches of song and small nonsense verses. Despite his indoor pallor and his deep-set, melancholy bird-like eyes, Jacob Sif is a good-humoured, kindly man, always ready with a humorous remark or a bit of fun such as is bound to awaken smiles and laughter in children and young housemaids, and always full of little surprises.

For instance, these delightful lucky dip packets that all children love so much: neat little blue envelopes with a glossy sticker on the outside and peppermints or liquorice inside – *plus* something. And this something is precisely the secret – it might be a tiny chirping flute, a ring with a pearl in it, a paper hat, a silver star made from tinsel or a black liquorice cat with ever such a delicate red bow around its neck.

Jacob Sif has his own small but loyal circle of customers made up partly of children, partly of older people who stick with him out of habit and because they know his story. Jacob Sif's story is no ordinary one. It can never quite be consigned to the past, and nor does it really belong there. For although Jacob Sif is only small and slight of build, a hollow-cheeked, worn man with purple, hairless hands, and although he is only of limited intellect with thoughts that are not particularly far reaching and feelings that are not particularly deep, he is a man whose life has a touch of the fairy tale: like a piece of crystal shining doggedly in the midst of a pile of everyday rubble, indeed a sunken treasure at the bottom of a turbid, murky ocean.

Jacob Sif was originally a little daydreamer, but life quickly taught him to prick holes in the useless soap bubbles of his dreams and make himself useful behind a counter. He was only fourteen when he became apprenticed to the lonely chandler Sofus Woolhand, a bearded, shaggy, but always clean and well-groomed man, whose view of the world was that dust and dirt are the root of all evil and so must be blown, swept, rubbed or scratched away wherever they are found.

From this Sofus, Jacob Sif had learned to blow dust away, to smooth things with the flat of his hand and to scrape with his thumb nail. In general, he went through a strict and petty-minded training in the kind of order and cleanliness that borders on the hateful and destructive. In other respects, too, the apprenticeship with Sofus Woolhand was a hard and uncomfortable time for Jacob, for the old chandler was incredibly tight-fisted and exposed both himself and his apprentice to the most incredible cold and deprivation.

And indeed, one beautiful day Sofus Woolhand actually died of cold. His apprentice – the only person with whom the eccentric old man consorted at that time – found him one morning frozen stiff at the worn and spotlessly clean kitchen table, with his hairy hand clutching his bankbook. Immediately behind him there was a paraffin stove that had run out of paraffin and a saucepan full of frozen salep. It was the morning of the third day of Christmas.

For eleven years now, Jacob Sif worked as an assistant in various shops and warehouses, slaving away from early morning until midnight. In time, he had saved so much from his wages that, with the help of a loan from his bank, he was able to buy Sofus Woolhand's neglected old house on Watchman Hill, where he started to trade on his own account. The house had in the meantime been in the hands of the unfortunate merchant Absalon Isaksen. Absalon had never had any great turnover; he had been sadly addicted to drink and was thought to have earned his living mainly on the sale of alcohol.

But in a dark corner up in the loft in the old building, the unhappy Absalon had left a biscuit box full of unpaid bills together with books revealing accounts that had never been rounded off. Among these there was also what was known as a ledger, which contained not a single numeral but was on the other hand full of old proverbs, sayings, ballads, sailors' songs and light-hearted ditties all written down in neat handwriting, and the new owner of the house often spent time with this book and came to value it highly.

Soon after Jacob Sif had taken over the little shop, he became engaged and married, and now we come to this remarkable chapter in his life, a piece simply taken out of the Arabian Nights in the midst of all the otherwise petty and trivial happenings by which he was surrounded.

Among Jacob Sif's first regular customers was an Icelandic family by the name of Jonasson who dealt in fancy goods and whose shop was situated further up the hill. The family consisted of a husband, wife and three daughters. These daughters were among the town's most highly praised beauties; they were effervescent in the way of Spanish women, big, proud and bold, and it goes without saying that they were much courted. The two oldest, Rosa and Lilja, had already been engaged several times, and the youngest and most beautiful, Viola, who was a little quieter by nature than the other two, had for some time been seen in the company of a good-looking and elegantly dressed man by the name of Hjaltalin, by all accounts an incredibly wealthy merchant who was visiting the town that summer.

However, this Mr Hjaltalin now completely disappears from the scene, and the incredible thing happens that this beautiful Viola goes and becomes Jacob Sif's wife.

It all started in a strange way in that Jacob fell wildly in love – not with Viola, but with a magic lantern that was exhibited in the fancy-goods-dealer's window.

It was love at first sight and completely irrevocable. There was something in the then twenty-seven-year-old grocer's heart that melted at the sight of the round, soft, colourful slide projected on to the white disc in Jonasson's window in the rain and the darkness of that miserable October evening, something that warmed him deep down in his soul and almost brought tears to his eyes.

This piece of magic was not cheap, and he couldn't

really afford it, but all considerations were a waste of time. Jacob Sif turned up the following day in the fancy-goods shop and bought the lantern.

It was Viola who served him, and they were alone in the shop. She taught him how to work it. She took him into a small room at the back of the shop, in which the window could be darkened by means of an internal shutter, and in the darkness here the magical spot stood out on the wall to show a submarine landscape of red and violet sea anemones, shining eels and rays, deep palm groves of seaweed and hanging spring-green veils of algae and dark corals.

Jacob Sif was so taken by all this colourful dream that he was scarcely aware of Viola. But later that evening, when he was sitting alone and again seeing the magical images of the bottom of the sea, he couldn't but feel quiet surprise at the thought of how obliging and sweet the young girl had been. Indeed, she had stood close to him in the dark, and he had felt her hair against his cheek and sensed the delicate perfume of her skin. And the way in which she had talked had been so sweet and friendly. Well, of course, the sweet thing had been a saleswoman, and she knew the art of persuading people to buy, something she had learned from her father, who was a very clever and smart businessman.

But when she came to buy two tins of meat balls the following day, Viola was to his surprise still as friendly and charming. She asked how he was getting on with the lantern; she gave him a warm look, and their eyes met almost tenderly – what was all this hocus-pocus really about? Perhaps she was making a fool of him. She presumably thought he was silly for buying the Magic Lantern. But, then, why did she stay? Why did she not go off and forget the whole thing now that the sale had been made once and for all and the goods paid for?

But Viola took her time, and as there were no other customers in the shop she and Jacob had quite a long conversation about this, that and the other, and the coquettish look of affection did not disappear from Viola's eyes. Jacob felt confused and anything but at ease; he burst into a sweat and made a series of clumsy remarks, and when Viola had finally gone, he hurried into the office to see in the mirror how foolish he really looked. Right enough, his cheeks were flushed and puffy, one eyelid was trembling idiotically and his mouth was smiling an alien, foolish smile. Jacob Sif was not accustomed to female company, and he had always felt ill at ease when together with ladies and well-to-do girls.

I suppose she thought it's such a pity for you, he thought with a sigh. She feels sorry for you because you are simply an innocent fool who bought her Magic Lantern and perhaps paid far too much for it, and here you are now playing with it at night.

And sadly, despondently and in some inner intoxication and madness, he recalls the young, pale blonde beauty with the intense blue eyes. This amazing girl had stood and as it were caressed her lower lip with her little finger and with her head a little on one side while submitting him to a warm and quizzical examination that seemed to emanate from some profound inner understanding.

"Rubbish." He dismissed it all and set about blowing at the counter and scratching away a little black stain with his thumb nail.

But the following evening, after closing time, something remarkable happened, something quite incredible, something completely unthinkable.

There stands Jacob Sif making up the till, when there

is a gentle knock on the little window in the door. He writes down the figure 87.37 so as not to forget it and goes across and looks out through the window. It's Viola. He lets her in. She is wrapped in a pale shawl. Her eyes are wild and demented. She says in a pleading voice,

"You must help me, Jacob. You must help me in my distress."

"*Do you hear?*" she adds almost threateningly and takes his hands.

Jacob Sif is dumbfounded. It's impossible for him to reply, impossible for him to make a sound. He hears the new pencil he had pushed up behind his ear fall to the ground with a tiny metallic sound and thinks, "There, that's fallen down."

He feels her hands and her arms; he allows himself to be led into the dimly lit little office and flops unresisting down on the lumpy oilcloth sofa from Sofus Woolhand's days. Silver dots and stars dance before his eyes, and he can't get the figure 87.37 that he wrote down out of his head again. He is aware of perfume and breath and of someone clutching at his arm and his hand. And a heartrendingly private and captivating voice:

"You've got to help me. I *won't* marry Hjaltalin! My parents are expecting me to, and so does he, but I *won't!* I can't stand him. I'm not interested in his money. He's been married twice before and besides he's just got married for a third time. He's so arrogant, a disgusting piece of work."

Jacob Sif feels warm tears on his hand. He suddenly recovers the power of speech.

"How do you think I might be able to help you?" he asks, completely flabbergasted.

"Well, couldn't we two get engaged?" Viola replies.

Her voice has suddenly grown calm. She presses his hand firmly and seeks to encourage him.

"I *have* already told my mother we are," she whispers tenderly in his ear. "So you mustn't let me down now."

"Well yes, but it'll never work," says Jacob, shuffling in despair. "No, please leave me now, Viola. You must be mad. You know, you're a ... no, you're perhaps the most beautiful girl in town; that's what everybody says, as I'm sure you know?"

He laughs long and foolishly.

"And as for me?" he adds and suddenly grows silent.

"And besides, I've heard he's got some incurable disease," Viola whispers.

A brief pause ensues, during which he can hear his watch ticking in his waistcoat pocket. "Ah," he thinks, "if only I were alone with this watch, with this tiny watch."

But now he suddenly finds himself embraced by soft arms, and he feels a large, loosely closed mouth seeking and touching his and slowly opening and breathing on him in a long, low sigh. She breathes and sighs in pain, like some stricken being; he feels something resembling repulsion, but this quickly gives way to a feeling of tender satisfaction. The darkness opens, full of secret hot springs, full of paradisiacal marine plants, submarine coral plants, live animals on stilts and with soft tentacles, kindly soft molluscs and crazy polyps, millions of years older than all human time.

Like a drowning man who to his unspeakable relief discovers that he is a fish, the little grocer Jacob Sif glides down into the depths of this eternal ocean and disappears in the blissful muddy world on the bottom.

Alas, that's all so far away now; it's more than twenty years in the past.

They married, and the little town was so overwhelmed

that its amazement found expression in a bon mot that is still
alive and often used:

> You make me squiff
> Like Jacob Sif!

Aye, the town was truly both astounded and confused, almost
unhinged, and of course evil tongues found plenty to talk
about, for it was damned well impossible to think of more than
one explanation: that Viola had allowed herself to be seduced
by that flashy show-off Hjaltalin and had chosen naive little
Jacob Sif to save her face.

But with a disdainful gesture, time overturned this
shameful theory, for the child did not come into the world until
eighteen months after the wedding. So there was nothing for it
other than to accept the facts and in bitter bewilderment note
that the ways of love are past understanding and the caprices
of the female know no limits or reason.

Indeed, it was contrary to reason and actually quite
shocking to see how the little grocer's family on Watchman
Hill seemed to flourish quietly, in happiness and comfort.

All this amazement and curiosity was also good for
trade; everyone had to go there and see this beautiful Viola
who spent her afternoons faithfully assisting her husband in
the shop, weighing sugar and flour and turning the handle
of the coffee grinder, was full of breezy comments and able
to use her eyes with great charm. And as for Jacob himself,
he put on weight and acquired a certain new authority in his
look, and he grew a moustache. He experienced a golden age.
Indeed, he felt so confident that he could actually be irritable
and demanding with his beautiful wife in the presence of
customers.

This proud age lasted for a whole three years, but then it came to a sudden end, for one day Viola left the country.

It was said that she was only going to visit her sister Rosa who meanwhile had married a solicitor in Copenhagen, and that she would only be away for about a month. But that month turned into two and then into three and in time to both six months and a whole year. For all this eternity, Viola kept fobbing her husband off with affectionate letters and fond assurances in which he ultimately no longer dared believe; and in time he himself had to cross the ocean to bring his confused wife back home.

Viola had fallen in love with someone else, and here Jacob Sif was unable to compete, for this was a very learned man with a fine position, a doctor, even a heart specialist.

Viola never came back to Jacob Sif and their little daughter. She had found a new and bigger world. Things had gone with them as they went with the girl and the merman, of whom one of the ballads written down in Absalon Isaksen's Ledger told:

> Indeed, 'tis so, and all is past
> No more we are as two,
> Alone I wander this world so vast
> Beneath the waters blue.
> There was none like you.

Jacob Sif had to accept the truth of this as he made for home again over the vast ocean and felt the dreadful leeches of loss boring into his breast. But perhaps this ending was for the best in spite of everything; it was at all events the only one possible.

Jacob Sif became resigned. He lacked the strength to nurture lasting sorrow or inextinguishable hatred, and he also lacked the perseverance to undertake profound reflection; he merely sank down into himself and slipped back into the old way of things as they had been before the change. He didn't become a sad man full of complaints; on the contrary, he adopted the habit of humming, whistling and singing ditties. He was always full of merry nonsense rhymes and meaningless sayings; he did his duty and maintained himself and his little daughter and also Trine the Eyes, who as time had passed had become an integral part of his home and made herself indispensable.

But every evening, when sleep announced its approach, Jacob Sif allowed himself to glide gently down into a veiled ocean of memories which as the years passed became increasingly unreal and amazing, memories of a happy death by drowning in waves of delight mingled with fear, memories of a nocturnal life in moonlight-green waters among suctorial molluscs and silent forests of living seaweed, filled with mermaidenly caresses and faint-inducing kisses.

Frost

Winter has arrived with frost and long, green hours of twilight. The Great War has finally finished, but Death is not yet satisfied with his profit from it and now he has mobilised epidemics and commanded them to visit every corner of the world and not to miss so much as the smallest bolt hole in the tiniest town in the most distant island in the ocean.

One of the effects of all this sickness will probably be to damage the Christmas trade, but then you have to put up with that and just hope for the best. Jacob Sif sighs as is befitting and hums absent-mindedly to himself.

> Christ is born of a virgin,
> We are not born to die,
> Tum tiddy tum tiddy my
> Aye, aye, aye aye.

It is Sunday afternoon, and Antonia sits helping her father make Christmas parcels and boxes. Jacob Sif's Christmas parcels are much in demand, partly because of their reasonable price and partly because there is just that little bit of *extra* about them, that inexplicable something. Something that can create an atmosphere and give pleasure. They are the products of a modest, but in its way quite profitable sale of applied art that father and daughter have built up over the years, and despite the most intense efforts, neither Salvesen the bookseller, Chamisso the pastry cook nor Ammon Olsen the prosperous draper have been able to cut them out of the Christmas trade.

Mother Pleiades

All attempts to copy or outdo Jacob Sif's lucky parcels are hopelessly crude and soulless. No one can compete with Antonia in making things out of coloured paper or nothing at all and creating the radiant and constantly changing borders and trimmings on these lids. And the secret ability fondly and ingeniously to invent their ever surprising contents is a skill denied to all human beings with the exception of Jacob Sif. A silence broken only by subdued humming and happy forgetfulness of self is mixed in the little living room with the scent of cardboard and glue.

> Gilded it was from stem to stern
> And then God's words no one did spurn
> Trarimma trum, de dum de dum

So hums Jacob Sif.

But in the dark room at the side, where the boy lies sleeping in his cradle, the new moon and stars of the primeval night hold sway; Orion's belt rises obliquely from the sea as in the dawn of creation and countless potentials breathe in their warm shawls. The stars twinkle intensely and impatiently in their longing for human eyes, yearning passionately for the great universal event to take place, for the hour to arrive when life opens its wondering eyes and *sees*. The distant suns complain; uncontrollable tempests of fire rage in their bellies; they protest cruelly in their blind isolation like women doomed to everlasting birth pains. But life nevertheless still finds itself in a state of passive slumber, and several aeons will pass before the sleepy eyes are opened and after a great deal of fear and trembling are finally filled with the kindness that sees, explains and helps, and which is the meaning and objective of existence.

"I must go down for some more glue," says Jacob Sif, getting up.

Out on the staircase he continues to hum his snippets of verse.

> Those mills are so well made
> We can't find better for toffee
> There's nothing better in the trade.
> They grind both cinnamon and coffee.

Antonia puts down the scissors and goes into the bedroom to attend to the little one in the cradle. He is sound asleep, and outside the stars are twinkling in the frost. Everything is as it should be. The world is resting and taking a pause.

But now Trine comes home, and so the peace is gone.

Trine the Eyes is a spirit of discord, a pessimist and a killjoy; alas, she is one of those unhappy virgins in the depth of whose heart the lamp refuses to burn, although it is constantly filled with the most exquisite oil of faith and self-denial. Indeed, she is one of those despairing creatures behind whose clean and polished integrity and altruism there lurks a restless destructive urge and a longing for death.

It is immediately obvious from the look on Trine's face that she comes with bad news. Well, since there is no avoiding it – let it only be Urania Mireta who has fallen in the slippery street and dropped a jar of jam and, at worst, sprained her ankle. Or, if it's to be something really bad, it could for instance be that Ammon Olsen's shop has burned to the ground – without anyone having come to any harm.

"*Napoleon* has died from Spanish flu," says Trine, giving Antonia a look that is completely on the side of death and Spanish flu.

At the same time, the little one in the cradle awakens and explodes in inconsolable complaint, and the quiet echo of a howl is transmitted throughout the universe just as happens when the ice cracks on a far distant lake.

"Napoleon was a decent man," Trine adds. "A man of faith. He's gone to his heavenly reward."

So everything is all right, really, and fortunately Trine's eyes calm down again for the time being. She goes out into the kitchen to make supper.

Antonia takes the child up from the cradle and puts him to her breast to settle him in the star-filled darkness, while she herself surrenders to a momentary pain.

"You are far too thin, Antonia. You should try some of this Brahma Elixir of Life that your father has in the shop." Or: "You are really incredibly stubborn, Antonia. It is not a good thing for you to be a greengrocer's daughter – you eat far too much *ginger*."

Napoleon Poulsen, the teacher, was fond of playing the part of one with superior knowledge and making his voice rasping and completely uninteresting. And at times Antonia would be in a defiant mood and refuse to be ignored, or she would deliberately give the wrong answer, completely and challengingly wrong. Indeed, like a shameless trollop she could sit and stare the teacher out with her blackish grey eyes, making him lose the thread and with a frosty smile allow her to go on. But long before she left school with good marks, he was profoundly and seriously interested in her and had her constantly in his thoughts.

For her part, Antonia very much liked her teacher and in the same way as the other girls in the class she was sorry for the quiet, twenty-six-year-old man with a mop of hair and sideboards because they knew that his fiancée had let him down and gone off with a telegraphist.

A year or so after she left school, Antonia became engaged to Napoleon. But even in the very first month of their engagement, it had become clear to her that she too would have to let him down. It was terribly sad to think of, and it hurt her deeply. But at the bottom of her heart, she knew that that was the way things would have to go.

Napoleon's room smelt of naphtha, leather and hair lotion. He didn't smoke. Above the bed, which was firmly covered with a dark rug, there hung some small framed portraits of Newton, Luther and Edison. Above the washstand there was a small medicine chest that Napoleon himself had made, and which contained shaving utensils, toothpaste, iodine, glove fingers, plasters, vaseline, bottles of antiseptic, camphorated oil and an ear syringe.

Napoleon had lots of books that he had personally bound in solid but drab black and brown covers. He read aloud for Antonia about Socrates, who was forced to drink a draught of poison, about the Emperor Nero, who made avenues of torches of the first Christians, about the Indian mathematician Aryabhata, who discovered the number pi and drew up the rules for extracting square and cubic roots, and about the great Pascal, the brilliant scientist who nevertheless put science aside in order to devote himself to the superior truths of the Christian religion.

To Napoleon's great surprise on the evening when he read about Pascal, Antonia suddenly burst into tears. He put the book down, and his voice trembled somewhere between concern and cheerful surprise:

"Oh, what is wrong, my love? Yes, it is ever so

exciting, is it not?"

He grasped her hands and laughed really heartily:

"Yes, but there now, my dear. I hardly think I have ever been so moved. It looks as though in a way you are even more open to cultural influence than I am. There, there ..."

Her sobbing became more and more hysterical; she turned vehemently away from him. She regretted her behaviour and felt ashamed at the idea that he thought her anger and sorrow had purely cultural causes. He kissed her tear-laden eyes and wiped her face with a handkerchief that smelt of pencil wood.

"Never," he said in a warm voice, "Never, Antonia, have I felt how profoundly we two belong to each other as I have done this evening."

Such was Napoleon, the first man in Antonia's life. He had many good qualities; he was a decent, considerate person, a man who understood his duty, and a man of faith, but at the same time he was insufferably egoistic, a tyrant of the quiet, terrible sort, one of those who are always in the right and so always feel they have been badly dealt with. Beneath his controlled kindness and attentiveness there was hidden a self-centredness that cried out to heaven. I personally and me personally were his eternal themes:

"I am not used to people taking me into consideration. I have learned how little my efforts are appreciated, and if people always ignore and hurt me, it is because they find it difficult to live up to the ideals I always keep before me. But I do not complain; I bear my burden with equanimity. No one in this world has been treated more abysmally than I have, but life taught me resignation at an early stage, and the best qualities in me have turned out to be strong enough to survive and live on and to enable me to combat any heinous machination directed against me."

Napoleon had brown eyes, fundamentally quite mischievous eyes, but the mischief in them never emerged; it was ice-bound once and for all. The handsome young man with the self-assured mien was one of those unfortunate beings to whom the ability to yield is totally denied. He had a profoundly and fatefully negative attitude to life and was doomed to perish in the wilderness of his self-centred world. He sought to explain this away both to himself and to her.

"And I do not make any demands on you, Antonia. I have not tied you to me so as to make use of you. You have your own free will in every respect; I am not playing irresponsibly with you; I am not seeking to make a fool of you, and it is not my intention that you should be my *harem*. But you can always be assured that whatever happens I am with you, for I really love you and feel that we belong to each other profoundly and indissolubly."

Napoleon looks at her full of dry satisfaction. On the tip of the little finger of his right hand there is a tiny pink sticking plaster emitting a slight antiseptic smell.

"And together with me you have the opportunity of extending your skills, of developing estimably and worthily and of building up a view of life that can be of lasting value and a source of constant joy and satisfaction to you. I do not dance with you, Antonia; I do not talk nonsense and make foolish remarks, for I consider you to be a person capable of developing, someone raised above frivolousness and already at home on a higher plane of life ... in contrast to my former fiancée, Inga, whose course of development unfortunately described an ever-descending curve."

Alas, that is how this poor, dry proponent of sorrow

and defeat was in the habit of talking to the girl he loved – just as the over-zealous snuffers talk to the burning wick, indeed as the extinguisher speaks to the living flame itself when it says, "I am smothering you to preserve you."

"For our animal nature, Antonia, the animal within us, will at all times attempt to assert itself and dominate us and drag us down to that level of animal ignorance from which we have had difficulty in emerging."

Thus spoke Napoleon Poulsen, and it was difficult to contradict him without appearing foolish. Once or twice she nevertheless almost managed to bring him to his knees and endanger his infallibility – not by means of words, but via a volcanic torrent of audacious caresses which he was unable to reciprocate. In sheer amazement he was put completely off balance and could not but forget himself; but this was only for a brief moment, and then he pulled himself mightily together and pushed her away, gently but resolutely.

"I think we are out of our minds, Antonia ... Let us not go so far as to anticipate marriage. Remember that you are not yet eighteen years old, and you are still rather backward for your age – physically speaking. I think you misunderstand me, my love. I have no wish to abuse the trust you show me; on the contrary, I wish to spare you and protect you, not least from yourself. Do you understand?"

On such occasions, Antonia felt a profound sadness mixed with a certain store of impotent fury bordering on hate. "Do you find me repulsive or something?" she thought. But she said nothing, simply withdrawing into herself and sitting with her head bowed while with her finger she drew on the melancholy, dark green plush of the table cover.

The great and final confrontation between Antonia and

Napoleon took place in his room one New Year's Eve and it was quiet but nasty.

The conversation had turned to Napoleon's first engagement, which he said had been nothing but one long period of humiliation to him. To which Antonia had passed the remark that it had perhaps also been a rather boring time for his fiancée, Inga.

He gave a start.

"What do you really mean by that?" he asked in a flat voice.

Antonia blushed and started examining her nails. A long silence ensued, during which the bells suddenly started ringing to welcome in the New Year. She understood that her words had had the effect of an ambush, a violent attack by robbers.

Finally, Napoleon cleared his throat and in a broken voice said, "Are you bored in my company, Antonia?"

It was a great effort for her to stay silent and not undo what she had just said. But she maintained her silence and she felt that this was itself a fresh mortal blow. She closed her eyes and kept her lips tightly closed.

A slight, almost silent and quite unexpected laugh made her look up, and she met Napoleon's laughing eyes. Yes, he was laughing. He was plainly rather amused and was applying his wit to the whole thing. He was quite calm and composed.

"Well, so that is one thing I know now," he said, putting both his hands down flat on the plush table cover. "Aye – I had been expecting it Antonia. It does not really come as a surprise."

His experienced smile was ironed out, and his face assumed an indulgent and relaxed expression.

"Good heavens," he said, throwing his head back. "Good heavens."

Antonia was close to tears. She regretted what she had done. How nicely and calmly he was taking it. What a shame it was for him really, she thought: "What a cruel person I am." Her heart was filled with sorrow and regret and an intense desire for reconciliation. However it ended, it must not end in *this* way. She had wanted to infuriate him, to see him rage and lose control of himself. But this quiet: "Good heavens!"...

She got up and went across to him tearfully and with her arms outstretched. But suddenly she froze from top to toe: he had raised a dismissive flat hand in the air, a quite calm and stiff hand, and his eyes had adopted an expression of thoughtful contempt.

"No scenes, Antonia, if you do not mind," he said imperiously. "Understand? Sit down quietly and let us talk things over."

He rose and started to walk to and fro.

"You see," he said, breathing deeply. "This situation is nothing at all new to me. You see, I have experienced one exactly like it with my previous fiancée Inga. In general, you two have quite a lot of things in common. You are both quite intelligent – relatively intelligent, if I may put it that way. And you both have the common feature that your intelligence relates entirely to superficial things and is not rooted in any real urge to educate yourselves further. As in the case with virtually all women, it is a kind of quasi intelligence, a feigned intelligence. You fool people who only see you from a distance. And your lack of intellectual depth corresponds to a certain kind of female instability, indeed a secret longing to sink *down*, in the direction of a proletarian animosity to all culture, down towards a crude animal level. Do you understand?"

He raised his eyebrows and gave her a smile that went right through her.

"I think that is why – that is why it is hopeless to attempt to raise you up, as for a time I persuaded myself it was possible to do, both in her case and now in yours. And as neither of you has succeeded in bringing me *down*, well, what then? Then the result is of course that we cannot find our way to a common position, do you not see?"

He stopped in front of Antonia and, without catching her eye, went on:

"And, my dear Antonia, if you are tired of me, then that is up to you. You have always had your freedom in relation to me. I have not tried to limit you in any way. I have not taken anything from you. I have not in any way tried to rob you of your dignity. I have not in any way *degraded* you. Nor am I asking you to leave me. I am merely noting that I have mistaken you."

Antonia felt immensely happy and relieved at these words, which were not to be misunderstood. She felt the urge to put her coat on and leave; indeed, she so looked forward to hurrying home down a street glistening with frost and to rejoicing in the fact that all her bonds had suddenly been broken. But at the same time, her eyes wept and her breast sobbed. She remained seated there, all hunched up, as though in regret, indeed as though in anticipation that he might take her back, however undeserved that was.

But he did not. He continued to walk to and fro, laughing quietly and humming to himself; he, too, seemed to be happy and relieved. In truth it was all a good thing. And the bells were ringing a new year in.

Finally, she wiped her eyes and cheeks and got up with a deep sigh. He helped her on with her outdoor clothes and formally shook hands with her. Goodbye, and Happy New Year.

Then why did she go back after getting half way home? Not because she regretted anything and wanted to re-establish the broken link. A sense of pity for him? Not that, either. The man had enough in himself. A certain feeling of being hurt at having been *rejected* in this way? But it was really she who had rejected him. Perhaps there was a certain curiosity at play; perhaps she wanted to be sure that he really was what he pretended to be and was not merely putting it on.

Antonia tiptoed noiselessly up the stairs and came to a halt in the corridor outside his door. She listened with bated breath. Had he perhaps gone out? Was he perhaps sitting there reading, quite unaffected and relieved after having liberated himself from her quasi intelligent encumbrance? Was she really such an encumbrance? Was she really so insignificant? Was it really so lovely to be free of her?

No, it was not. To her relief, but a relief mixed with sorrow, she heard a prolonged, tearful sigh, muffled by bedclothes. Then a new sigh and the clear sound of a breath being drawn by someone weeping. Her eyes filled with tears and she sobbed as she went down the stairs again, out beneath the New Year stars. Her warm breath made tiny, light, fleeting clouds in the clear frosty half-light.

The Able Seaman

The ship arriving at Christmas was laden with apples and nuts, mandarins and grapes, Chinese pistols and Bengal lanterns, fluted wax candles in all the colours of the rainbow, figs and carobs and lots more of these overseas wonders that had not been in the shops for many years, but had now once more been carried across the war-ravaged ocean. And Jacob Sif's shop is filled with sweet scents and in the midst of the bitter, anaemic winter is radiant like a stall in some Eastern fairy tale.

And as one element in this list of glorious things, there is for Antonia a striped envelope bearing a strange stamp; it has come from some hot country and contains two coloured postcards. One of them shows an Indian pagoda among palm trees, the other three brick-red, smiling dancers in colourful costumes.

Good heavens, it's a sign of life from *Peter* – how kind of him! Since he was last heard from, he has crossed the oceans and sailed down tropical rivers and as good as been at war; he has been bitten by some animal, the name of which it is impossible to read, and he has been ill in some hospital, and finally he has had to swallow a diamond to escape death – if any of this is to be believed. There are lots of girls here like those in the picture, the message concludes, but there was no one like you, you must believe me.

Antonia can only smile at this assurance, which comes to her from some inconceivable distance and always refers to her in the past, as though she were already dead and gone. It's so far away now, so past and done with.

But – *there was no one like you*. She, too, can say the same, and so she does, whispering and alone and with her eyes closed.

There was no one like *him*, as long as it lasted, even though it's over now, once and for all. It's wonderful to look back on, and so it always will be, but it's also terribly upsetting if you try to get to the bottom of it; indeed it can still quite well lead to tears and sleepless hours at night.

Scarcely a year after the breach with Napoleon, the enchantment of being deeply in love came into Antonia's life, the ruthless fire that is devoid of reason and thought, only an all-consuming need for tenderness and merciless determination.

You were so beautiful, Antonia, during the difficult time when your young love was blossoming ... no striking beauty, admittedly, no radiant film star, for you were not at all radiant; on the contrary, there could be something dusty and grey about you, something almost chilly and shadowy. You were neither fair nor dark, but pale and ashen blonde with dark grey eyes, thin and spectral, but finely built and with fully developed limbs that ended in wonderfully supple and firm hands and feet. You had an elegant walk and your movements were so distinguished. And it must also be said that in many respects you had remarkable gifts – you were a rare instrument on which to express longing and a passionate hunger for life; you were a violin of the noblest ilk, a dusty Stradivarius left behind in a distant corner of the world, but filled with secret power and with a superb potential for happiness.

The poor teacher and pedant Napoleon possessed none of the qualities that could liberate one's happiness. But on the other hand, that impossible Peter the gravedigger's son did, scatter-brained, untrustworthy and self-indulgent able seaman and layabout as he was. He possessed the breath that could produce a flame capable of making your mind's misty Pleiades burst into a warm glow; he could awaken your slumbering need to bestow profound sympathy and maternal devotion.

It all started one Sunday evening when, on her way home from the dance hall, Antonia was pursued by Peter, who had acquired some Dutch courage and now made a determined effort to enfold her in his embrace. She had no difficulty avoiding him, and she could easily have dodged inside the front door, but instead she remained on the doorstep and allowed herself to be embraced and kissed by him in the dense fog. She stroked his stiff, damp hair and whispered gentle words in his ear. She had always rather liked this strapping lad with the weak mouth and desperate eyes that looked as though they had sold themselves to the powers of evil. There was something fascinating about the fact that he was completely outside the rule of law and everyday respectability, that he was so fundamentally different from a Napoleon, and that he was simply called Peter. And then that he was so generally looked down on and feared.

The other point about this curious sinner was that he was a childhood friend of Orfeus Isaksen, Eliana the Ferrywoman's splendid son, who was now a violinist in Copenhagen. The two friends could always be seen together during the summer while Orfeus was home on a visit, and during all that time Peter had worn his Sunday clothes and done everything he could to behave well and look decent. And Peter was also a good musician, even though he only played a Jew's harp and an accordion.

"You're a bit of all right," said Peter encouragingly. "Now you just come with me and you'll see a bit of fun ..."

He took her arm, and they walked a short way

together, but then she grabbed the opportunity to dodge away from him. Through the window in the door she could see his brooding and searching figure outside in the dark. Now, with some difficulty, he lit a cigarette; the flame from the match illuminated his poor handsome but distorted features. He fell back against the fence that surrounded Chamisso the pastry cook's garden and stayed there dangling with his elbows pushed in through the bars like one who has been crucified.

"Perhaps he'll hang there like that all night," she thought. "Perhaps I ought to go out and help him to get off the fence."

But now he managed to free himself without assistance and drifted away in the fog, lonely and lost, like a disabled old ship on a treacherous ocean.

That night, Antonia lay awake for a long time, staring into the thick darkness. Funny snatches of verse from Absalon Isaksen's ledger kept resounding in her ears; in time they came together into a poem, and now she couldn't get rid of this ditty, which occupied her mind completely and made her go all hot and cold.

> And were you but a robber bold
> Upon the ocean cold,
> I would love you even so
> And plight my troth to you
> My turtle dove
> 'tis you I love
> But you do not love me.
>
> And even if you now should raise
> Your flag all black before my gaze

I still would love you even so
And plight my troth anew.
My turtle dove
'tis you I love
But you do not love me.

And if they took you and at last
Should hang you from your highest mast
Yet would I love you still my dear
Though then I'd have but little cheer.
My turtle dove
'tis you I love
But you do not love me.

The relationship between Antonia and Peter did not shock anybody, for the two lovers only met in deepest secrecy. They wandered off on distant paths across the heath that surrounded the town or along the deserted shore, and when it rained or snowed, they sought shelter beneath some eaves or in a boathouse near the harbour.

One evening, he took her into the churchyard, where Lukas the gravedigger had a small shed for his spades and pickaxes. There was also a rickety bench in there and an old oil cooker that could provide a little light and heat. Outside, in the wintry garden of the dead there was a whisper of withered grass and dry leaves. The emptiness and cold horror of death seeped into the little hut, and they were both afraid of the dead and of each other. But he sought to hide his fear behind shameless chatter and stories of ghosts, and she went along with this comedy, clinging to him and allowing him to calm her down until the heat of their bodies had forged its shell around them and shut all fear out.

Peter also had another place of refuge. One evening he picked the lock on one of Hansen's old warehouse doors and took Antonia up countless stairs to a little room at the very top, up in the loft, which was almost full of bundled herring nets. There was a tiny window. Outside the moon was shining on the waves of the sea. In this attic, perfumed with bark, raised high above the world and outside time, they had their first intimate union.

By nature, able seaman Peter was in no way the evil, demonic seducer that the well-meaning but blinkered psychologists of a later age have sought to make him. No, it was in reality our good Antonia with her vibrant, passionate personality who led the way in this love affair. So obediently and devotedly did she listen to the profusion of far too obviously tall stories and boasts which he retailed in order to conceal his secret self-contempt that he sometimes felt it was almost too much of a good thing and it aroused his sympathy and his urge to protect her.

"You're far too good for this world, Antonia. Good heavens above. Just think if you'd fallen into the hands of some really nasty scoundrel."

"I love you," said Antonia, filled with a secret sense of triumph.

Peter gradually stopped boasting of drastic experiences on his travels, of conquests and achievements. Instead, he went to the opposite extreme, indulging in boasting of a very different sort, revealing the innermost recesses of his rascally heart and making it look blacker than it was. But she let him talk as he wanted; she really never paid much attention to what he said, deafened and blinded as she was by the novelty and grandeur of her experience, the deep intoxication of a passion that was profound, unthinking and silent.

And later, when she was alone with her own thoughts, she closed her eyes and as though in deep prayer recited the verses from the old love song in Absalon Isaksen's ledger. Alas, this desperate ditty was like a vase that was precious but cracked. And the same applied to Peter, too. Despite his strength he was fragile; dependability was an unknown concept to him, and she well knew that their love was also without dependability and wouldn't last.

And like all women who are deeply in love, she wept tears both bitter and sweet at the thought of her separation from her love, and brave tears at the premonition of a more lasting and richer love that was to come, a love unbounded and rounded like the earth, as incomprehensible in its power as the night and the day.

Hence the quiet smile with which you finally fall asleep, Antonia, with your mouth half open, like one obediently following a call that is full of promise.

There was only one of Peter's many tall stories and confused accounts that really caught Antonia's attention sufficiently for her to remember it later. This was the story of the forgotten store of soap and perfume.

This exquisite collection of samples was kept in a large, whitewashed warehouse room with ogival windows. It belonged to a foreign soap agent who had gone off and left it all behind and appeared to have forgotten all about it for more important matters abroad. At the age of fourteen, Peter found his way into this wonderful cave and stayed there for a while. It was all so lonely and undisturbed that he could both sing songs and chant melodies, indeed shout if he wanted to without being noticed by anyone at all.

At first, he merely went around and sniffed at the fine wares, which were beautifully and temptingly arranged on long tables with wooden trestles under, irritated that the delightful green and pink bottles didn't contain sweet beverages, and that the lovely marzipan-coloured hand soaps couldn't be eaten.

To get something out of it nevertheless, he reluctantly sprinkled eau de cologne on his clothes, spread brilliantine on his hair and rubbed his hands and face with an array of creams. He kissed and cuddled a life-size cardboard advertisement representing a kitchen maid exclaiming in delight at some sort of polish, and he coloured her cheeks dark red with lipstick making her look as though she was ashamed.

But all this was strangely futile and disappointing. He languished with a sense of loneliness, deprivation and gnawing regret in the midst of all this overpowering perfume, and he gave a sigh of relief every time he left this confoundedly stupid cave again. But driven by some irresistible urge he went back day after day and in despair abandoned himself to the hair and skin care he had embarked on. He sampled the contents of the bottles; they all tasted like gall and wormwood, but he nevertheless had to try them all with his tongue for the sake of his peace of mind.

In desperation he finally had the idea of taking up some chocolate, macaroons and cigarettes that he bought for the money he earned as an errand boy for Ammon Olsen. He ate and smoked until he felt terribly sick, threw up in a packing case filled with wooden shavings, prayed to God, twisted contritely in the dust on the damp floor and abandoned himself to howling impotently in sorrow and pain.

"And what then, Peter? How did it all end?"

"End?" Peter hesitated as though he had already said enough, and she thought to herself that it had probably ended with some terrible retribution.

"Well," he said at last tossing his head and curling his mouth into the warm, irresponsible smile of a story-teller endowed with rather too much imagination, "Of course, it ended with me smashing it all up. I took the bottles as targets and threw all the soaps at them. Then I took a crowbar that was lying up there and smashed all the bottles I'd missed; and in the end I took the cardboard girl and knocked holes in her and chopped her head off. By that time it was all in such a hell of a mess that I couldn't persuade myself to go there any more."

Of course, the relationship between them was discovered. Trine the Eyes was not slow to act; she had her net out for him, and she zealously hauled her catch in. And then there was a row:

"You, a pretty, sensible girl, and a poor old father's only daughter and hope for the future, and then a lad like him, a cheeky, irresponsible windbag and cheat, a miserable good-for-nothing and thief. To think that we should have such a dreadful disappointment!"

Trine fumed and raged; she prayed and implored and expressed her scorn and horror in sombre laughter that went right through anyone listening. Jacob Sif hung his head and sighed, but otherwise said nothing – Trine, of course, said everything there was to say on that subject, and more as well. She threatened Antonia with the priest, the doctor and the children's officer and she talked of the church's right and duty to interfere and of God's just punishment.

"I know all about sin, Antonia, believe you me, I've seen it close to, and I know its fruits, for the wages of sin is death, as it is written. Do you understand, you foolish little creature: *death*! Do you understand now? No, you don't, for if you did you certainly wouldn't have smiled."

Trine turns away in desperation. She collapses on to a chair and sits rocking to and fro with clasped hands pressed to her cheek.

"Trine," says Antonia timidly, touching her hand.

Trine looks up. There is for once no strength in her eyes, and she is completely crushed. Antonia kneels before her and clutches her hands. She hears her murmur in an affectionate, husky voice that has a devastating effect on her:

"Antonia, you are *my* child after all, aren't you? It is us two, you know, Antonia ... I am your mother, aren't I?"

"Yes." Antonia nods and shudders at the untruth.

And she surrenders to Trine as she has surrendered a thousand times before, surrenders in the same way as the pilgrim surrenders to the storm. And they both know it and it distresses them both, but things have never been any different and they never will be any different.

Antonia felt sorry for Trine and for her father, but nevertheless especially for Peter, who was so unreasonably being condemned. She made no attempt to contradict Trine, but she put up with her merciless criticism, and she allowed herself to be persuaded to apply for the vacant job in Salvesen the bookseller's office, which was part of the effort to get her established in new and better company so that she might have some different ideas. She went so far in her cunning compliance that she went a couple of times together with Trine to the parish hall to hear the strict evangelical Pastor Ryvingsen rage and foam against the judgmental sectarianism of the Plymouth Brethren and Seventh Day Adventists. She was prepared to make any sacrifice that could placate the ferocious forces that sought to undermine her love and destroy her happiness.

But it was all in vain. There was no fooling Trine; she saw through the act; she was not to be satisfied with a half-hearted approach, and as there was plenty of evidence that the degrading, sinful relationship between the two young people continued in secret, she personally went to see the seducer and gave him a piece of her mind.

Peter, who was otherwise able to give as good as he got if anyone went for him, felt curiously weak and ineffectual when faced with this all-consuming woman with the eyes. He adopted quite the wrong approach and started to deny that he had had anything to do with the girl.

"We've been walking out a bit," he said. "And that's all."

But Trine turned out to be devilishly well informed. She could almost recite the date and hour of every aberration. She cited witnesses by their full names, so there was no getting around it. She finally threatened him with the law, for there was also talk of his having broken into someone else's property, and if the law was once brought into it, there were old and absolutely reliable lists of misdeeds to bring up both here and there.

In the face of this barbed ruthlessness, Peter felt quite defenceless; his answers lost all their power and disintegrated into embarrassing generalities and patently obvious white lies. He finally came to a halt and felt himself almost to be a man of culture in the face of this odious and scurrilous woman. And indeed, she finally forced him to utter the words she had come to hear and pass on:

"And when all's said and done, I can't see how Antonia is as wonderful and priceless as you say, Trine, for she's no different from most girls ... and there are plenty to choose from, so just you keep your little lass. I won't come any more; you can be sure of that. And by the way, you can tell her that I've signed on with the *Garm* to go to Spain today. And then, take my advice and get out and don't tempt me to help you on your way with this ...!'"

Trine looked at his threatening fist with a tired little smile. She looked almost to have been placated as she withdrew from the young man she had just overpowered.

As far as Peter is concerned, this little affair is at an end, and a good thing too. Just like any other little affair of the same kind it was bound to finish sooner or later in any case. And that was that. Life is long, the waves are shining and distant shores beckon. A good bit of medium-sized game has been brought down, an agile young seal, quite a good catch. And afterwards, the bold hunter has got it in the neck for poaching; he's been buried under a pile of reprimands from a daft old woman. But of course, he'd held his own pretty well and maintained his dignity as a man of the world in the face of this small town monster.

All right, Peter, let's say that, and just you go and paddle your young canoe and hide your wounds beneath an elegant dressing of fresh boasts. Take out your accordion and forget Trine's eyes and the painful injuries she's subjected you to with her words. Once more you've been told you're the son of that dismal drunkard Lukas the gravedigger and that in return for coffee, kind words and discarded children's clothing your mother used to empty fine folk's night soil out at dead of night and return the buckets nice and clean.

You can picture her as she comes stealing along on her poor, furtive errand, decent and dutiful, unending devotion reflected in her eternally kind and gentle face with a cheekbone decorated in every colour of the rainbow after the inebriated gravedigger's last violent attack. She carries a bucket in each hand and dodges from the corner of one house to the next in this filthy old sewerless town until, without being discovered, she has reached the cliff from which human ordure is thrown into the sea – a hellish place full of rats and snakes, the demeaning stench of which you knew in your childhood and still have in your nose like the evil breath of a bad conscience. During your dog watches out on the restless ocean, you have raged and wept at the thought of how alone she was during these hours in the night, this gentle soul who brought you into this world, while the self-satisfied brood, which didn't find it beneath their dignity to fill the buckets but certainly beneath their dignity to empty them, lay snoring contentedly beneath their duvets.

Play on, dear Peter, and try to forget her exhausted figure when she got up during the night and prepared for these humiliating excursions when, well disguised in her grey scarf, she put out the kitchen lamp and disappeared into the darkness. And try, too, to forget and to sing away the fact that at the bottom of your heart you can't forgive yourself for not giving her a helping hand or siding with her against her violent husband, but you lay there instead dreaming of how you would give her golden days and raise her gloriously into the light when *your* time came.

And now that she's old and sick, it's too late. Aye, all those things you were going to avenge and fulfil cry out to you and are unachieved. You found no gold or diamonds; you were not even allowed to go ashore in countries where such precious things were to be found; there were sentries everywhere and secret police, preparations for war and fear of spies, and you would never have had the strength or courage to turn into a scoundrel in the grand style – on the contrary, you allowed yourself to be cheated by a lousy clock dealer in Leith!

Too late? Well, that might well be asked. It's rather that you haven't yet made a start. Get going – and you'll see you can if only you pull yourself together and get away from this hole. You've hung around like a complete fool here for long enough, going around with a girl, that daft little Jacob Sif's peculiar daughter who's fallen for you hook, line and sinker. And to be honest, you for your part have stuck to her far too much as well. Aye, you were well on your way to getting bogged down in this miserable little place for the rest of your life.

But now you've got rid of her quite painlessly.

Peter purses his lips to produce a final whistle as he throws down the accordion.

All this about already having signed on for the *Garm* – well, of course it wasn't entirely true, but just a boast he flung in Trine's face. He hasn't signed on at all; he's only gone gallivanting around and drinking a bit with his friend Harald and having his dates with Sif's Antonia in the evenings.

On the other hand, it really *is* possible to sign on for the old tramp steamer, which is about to go to Cardiff and then further off into the wide world. So it's a question of whether to go on it or not, and so it's a case of constantly weighing up the pros and cons, as it always is when there is freedom of choice. His mother has asked him, begged him, to stay at home until the war is over and the submarines are gone. But that might take years yet.

And then there's still that crazy girl Antonia. It's not all over with her, not by any means.

Up and down, this way and that way, the tooth-ache

of indecision can't be deadened by playing the accordion or whistling or yawning aloud.

He drifts down to the harbour to find out more about the *Garm*. To his discomfort, he discovers that the old crate is due to sail this very evening and that Harald has pulled himself together and signed on as an apprentice navigator. But there's still a job for an able seaman.

Harald, who is going around happily after having a few drinks in anticipation, is the one who puts an end to the indecision. Of course, it'd be a hell of a mistake if he didn't make short shrift of it and take this chance. And regret, which always sticks its snotty nose out when something has become irrevocable, can very deservedly have its snout biffed by Harald's bottle. So goodbye, Mother, and that's that. And as for Antonia, a short farewell letter composed to the accompaniment of laughter in the company of friends, but written down when he is on his own to the accompaniment of subdued sniffing, for now, at the last moment, she is no longer only a girl you've come across, but she has achieved the rank of the very girl in your life, the one who will always be a painful memory to you.

And whatever you can otherwise find to boast about when the tempestuous waves of self-contempt have to be stilled with the oil of unashamed bragging, you will nevertheless long be reluctant to boast about this quiet, radiant maiden who was like wax in your hand.

Evil

There are many rumours circulating concerning Eggertsen, the treacherous preacher and runaway embezzler, but unfortunately they contain a host of strange contradictions: there are those who maintain that Eggertsen has been arrested in America and imprisoned in Sing-Sing, while others insist that he has joined that infamous Mormon sect, the one that goes in for polygamy, and that he has abandoned poor Jutta Chamisso and left her to her own devices. Indeed, there are also those who suggest that he has sold her to the white slave trade.

But then, what about the sorely tried congregation of Plymouth Brethren? Has it collapsed in ignominy and regret, brought down by Eggertsen's unparalleled betrayal?

No. On the contrary, it is now prospering better than ever and has long ago reverted to its curious old form of public entertainment.

A new man has come in place of Eggertsen. He is called Nimrod Smith. He is a Scot and the agent for the world-famous Albion raincoats, and he wins everyone over with his gentle manner, his bizarre broken language and his wonderful skill at playing the accordion. His bright and cheerful way of speaking has the effect of healing all wounds; he is also a learned man who knows the whole of the New Testament by heart and never gets mixed up when quoting chapter and verse, and he introduces new hymns full of consolation and triumph.

Aye, this little man with his red beard captures all hearts; he wins new adherents and brings back those who have lapsed. Ammon Olsen, the draper, who left the congregation in fury and exasperation, has been so placated by the new preacher that he has returned and been baptised afresh. Young Nimrod has regular access to his splendid house and is said to be half engaged to his daughter Elizabeth. And Ammon Olsen has acquired the sole rights to Albion overcoats and all other Albion products.

Nimrod Smith does not fulminate in the way that Eggertsen used to do. He goes around wearing a kilt and with bare knees, and he is infinitely gentle and easily moved to smiles or tears. "All through grace" is his motto.

Trine the Eyes and Urania Mireta have been across to hear this man Nimrod preach, and Trine returns with her eyes reflecting the most profound scorn.

"They sing waltzes and play dance music," she says. "Ugh! And then he smiles and curtseys like a woman! Whatever else can be said about the scoundrel, Eggertsen was at least a man!"

"Yes, he was certainly a man," confirms Urania Mireta dreaming unpleasant dreams.

Jacob Sif has a far-away look in his eyes and is drumming on the table with his fingers.

"Well, no one asked you to go there, Trine," he says quietly.

Trine ignores him and continues her angry outburst in a loud voice.

"And then all that about grace and forgiveness provided you have a dip in that horrible stuffy bath of theirs. Oh no, it's not *so* easy to escape the wages of sin."

"No, the wages of sin," repeats Urania Mireta, shaking her head and looking nervously at Trine.

But not everyone has forgotten Eggertsen and his misdeeds. The mercurial pastry cook Chamisso swears a dear and sacred oath in Italian to the effect that vengeance will strike the *poveraccio*, and that poor Jutta shall surely be snatched from his claws.

"Just you wait," he says. "Scotland Yard has the matter in hand! *Scotland Yard non molla tanto facilemente!*"

Chamisso bends down, angrily jerks open the trapdoor in the floor and wild-eyed and with features turned to stone he disappears down into the cellar and its aromas of cakes and biscuits.

"You do think we'll get Jutta back safe and sound, Trine?" asks Mrs Chamisso, earnestly clutching Trine's hand.

"We can hope and pray," replies the sibyl.

"Jutta was always such a quiet, dependable girl," says Mrs Chamisso. "I don't understand it at all. We didn't like her going to Eggertsen's meetings. We were afraid she'd have her head turned. But that it was going to end *this* way ...!"

Trine gathers a few cake crumbs in her hand, delicately sucks them up into her mouth and washes them down with coffee.

"Yes," she says emphatically. "The world is evil, Mrs Chamisso. Sin is evil. It *hurts*."

"Yes, sin is evil," echoes Urania Mireta with a deep sigh.

Nice Mrs Chamisso encounters Trine's eyes and turns away weeping.

And there you sit now, Trine, and have no idea how to deal with this worry and this maternal grief. Instead of opening, your heart closes, and you are completely at a loss. For surely you came to help and comfort poor Mrs Chamisso, not to increase the burden of her misery?

There are very mixed opinions about Trine the Eyes. She is something of a mystery; her past is unclear and bound up with legend. She is said not to have been without a certain responsibility for the unhappy death of a certain Doctor Tulinius. There are those who call her *Evil Trine* in the belief that she has the evil eye and can invoke a curse on people she doesn't like. She is also known as the *werewolf*. Her dark eyebrows grow into one and have the look of a black bat with its wings spread. She is also said to have a spiteful tongue. Take care of Trine's good wishes, for they are disguised curses, people say.

But if Trine is evil, why does she visit the sick and the old and knit woollen underclothing for poor children? Why does she come and comfort and feed the three helpless Schibbye old maids? And why – more or less with the approval of Jacob Sif – has she undertaken responsibility for supporting both Urania Mireta and old Blind Anna?

Urania Mireta, the daughter of the late rose painter Pontus, lived alone in her father's dilapidated house and was ill and deaf and almost eaten up by lice when Trine took her in hand. Few others would have done that.

There are many who say that Trine is a wonderful woman. And yet these people who heaped praise on her were perhaps also among those who chose to lock their doors when they saw her approaching.

Trine is in a curious situation. It has fallen into the lot of this determined and tough old maid to become an unpopular figure feared by many people.

When, almost a generation ago, Trine the Eyes came to town from the distant little village by the fjord, where she had grown up, she was a well-built, pretty young woman in her early twenties with big, searching eyes. Doctor Tulinius jokingly called her *The Haughty Dame*.

The doctor's surgery was a large house with high-ceilinged rooms which echoed when people spoke. And when the doctor's wife sat at her grand piano the house resounded with singing and tumultuous whirlwinds of notes. The doctor's wife had not taken her husband's name, but was known as Helga Aho. She was of Swedish or Finnish descent and a trained concert singer.

Madam Helga rarely got up before the morning was well advanced, and she never undertook any form of domestic work. She employed a capable elderly cook to prepare the food, and Trine's job was to keep the upstairs and downstairs rooms in good order. The doctor was a portly man with a heather-like, curly beard and deep-set eyes beneath bushy brows. He was in his mid-thirties. His wife, who was some ten years younger, had white skin, green eyes and hair the colour of claret. She was intense and unpredictable by nature, sometimes irascible and unreasonable and sometimes kindly, cheerful and informal. There was no one who could be as childishly unjust as Madam Helga, and no one so genuinely and fervently contrite. She often talked to Trine, whom she was fond of praising and spoiling and to whom she was forever giving new names.

"We'll have to put a bit of life into you, Isolde," she said. "You look a bit down in the mouth, longing for your Tristan, your liberator, who is so far away from here. You dream about him every night, Isolde; he comes surreptitiously, pale with love, like a spirit, like a ghost ..."

And Helga asked embarrassing questions about this Tristan, whom she herself had invented, so poor Trine blushed and wished she could sink into the ground.

"Does he really love you? Does he go down on his

knees to worship you? Does he crush you? Can he warm you so much he makes you cry out?"

And she showed the terrified girl how you cry out and carry on and surrender, breathless and with closed eyes and quietly sobbing as though in great sorrow and suffering.

At other times, Madam was morose and impossible to please, especially when she had had something to drink at a party. Great quantities were drunk in the doctor's house, not only when they had guests, but also as part of everyday life. The doctor and his wife always had wine with their dinner and often continued with stronger drinks after the meal. They could sit throughout the evening and night, celebrating, just the two of them. It was not unknown for Trine to find the doctor lying stretched out on the floor at six o'clock in the morning. He would get up shivering when she woke him and then, with his teeth chattering, he would drink his morning coffee and wash it down with a glass of cognac.

"Don't look at me with those eyes, Trine," he would say, cheerfully waving her away.

Trine thought the doctor's drinking terrible and in the secret recesses of her soul she prayed to God to forgive him for his sinful life and guide him to better ways.

Trine came from a God-fearing home out in the country, and even to this day her heart is filled with turmoil and horror when she thinks of the harsh, godless life that was lived in Doctor Tulinius's home and of the grim fruits of retribution to which this life gave rise. Quite innocently and entirely against her will, she was whirled into this devilish game that evil powers forced upon the unfortunate doctor and his wife, and she was swept into playing a part in the terrible, sad events that were the final outcome of that game.

In spite of his fondness for strong drinks, Doctor Tulinius was anything but weak and negligent. He had an iron constitution and attended to his work, both in his surgery and in the hospital, and he was not one to make difficulties when sent for at an inconvenient time. It happened more than once that, by boat or by horse, often at dead of night and in bad weather, he left some festive gathering so as to go to the help of a sick person or someone who had had an accident. And this willingness and helpfulness also ensured that he was generally liked, indeed more than that: he was loved and idolised.

His wife, on the other hand, did not exactly enjoy people's favour; she was widely disliked; people found her affected, and there were many who believed she was an evil spirit who did her husband more harm than good.

"You hate me as well, Trine," Madam Helga said one day. She lay in bed taking it easy, although it was getting on for midday. "You all hate me. Because you love *him*. Everyone loves him and hates me."

She suddenly sat up and focused her green eyes on Trine's:

"Why? Because you're stupid and lack any sense of culture. You're all of you poor sheep whose only concern is how best to get rid of your tooth-ache and stomach-ache and all your other aches and pains. And when I play the piano it's merely making enough din to give you ear-ache; and singing's just the same as howling, isn't it? Robert Schumann and Heinrich Heine – who were they, Trine? They were nothing at all, of course. But the priest who tends your miserable souls, and the doctor who fills your terrified stomachs with bismuth, well, now they are folk worthy of respect."

Trine tossed her head as she withdrew with madam's untouched breakfast.

"Trine," Helga shouted peremptorily. "Do you know what he is, your idol, this great doctor? He's a wolf. An executioner. Oh, I could tell you things about him that would make you want to sink into the ground."

Madam Helga leant back in her cushions, sighed deeply and stared at Trine as though in great distress and helplessness.

"Come over here, Trine," she whispered. "Put the tray down and come over here and let me hold your hand. You're such a strong girl, and you're just the right one for *him*. Do you realise that? Yes, Trine, you are. He says so himself."

Trine put her free hand up to her face and bowed her head deep to hide her blushes and embarrassment.

"Aye. Just see how infatuated you are with him," said Madam Helga with a scornful laugh. "And how lovely it would have been, Trine, if you were expecting a baby with him now. Wouldn't it, Trine? How you'd go and look forward to it and hold your stomach and count the days."

She flung Trine's limp hand down and started moaning softly. Trine made to get up, but her mistress grabbed her arm again and forced her down on the edge of the bed once more:

"But for me, Trine," she whispered in a deeply confidential voice, "For me it's a terrible misfortune. You don't understand. But that's how it is. I daren't and won't carry his child. I could die as a result, 'cause I'm not strong. But that wouldn't matter all that much. I could lose my voice as a result. It could turn rough and cracked, like a broken bell."

Madam Helga made her voice sound hoarse and ugly and went on, "Listen. That's how Doctor Tulinius's wife speaks, that fat, sated woman with the baby at her breast. She's no longer Helga Aho. She's a much maligned poor woman who's been seduced."

And now Madam got up and assumed her real voice again. Grinding her teeth and once more pushing the girl away, she shrieked,

"But that's not going to be, that's not going to be. Helga Aho shall not be destroyed and silenced and dragged down into oblivion and destruction. Get away from me, you little devil, and hate me as much as you like, insignificant bit of fluff that you are. No, forgive me, Trine. I didn't mean what I said. You are not insignificant; on the contrary, you are a beautiful girl, *beautiful*, aye – you could be a Spanish girl, so you could. And your eyes are wonderful. And they're not as serious as they seem … they don't really say the same as your lips speak; they go their own secret way. I think you're a sort of seductress, Trine, aren't you?"

Madam Helga let out a strange, sharp laugh:

"But you've got dough in your soul instead of fire, so you have."

Trine said nothing, but thought to herself, "Better to have the leaven of faith in my soul than the fire of sin." And she remembered the text in which Jesus somewhere talks approvingly of the leaven.

That afternoon saw the start of a dull and ominous quarrel between the doctor and his wife. A subdued tempest of harsh and hateful words could be heard through the half-open door to the bedroom, and Trine, who was on her way up to her room came to an involuntary standstill on the stairs and listened, not in order to eavesdrop, but because she was afraid that the two mad folk would do harm to each other.

"A murderer, that's what you are," she heard Madam Helga's furious, threatening words. "And if you don't help me, I'll take my own life, for I've got a right to do that. So now you know."

"You know no shame, Helga," he replied, his voice low with scorn or pain. "But you shall have your way. Then afterwards you can sit there and languish and sing the Wiegenlied! And Aladdin's cradle song. Yes, Helga, just you sing it, just you sing it."

"No, you're out-devilling the Devil himself," she suddenly cried out aloud and broke into a harsh laughter that shook Trine so deeply as she listened that the tears welled up and blinded her eyes.

"You," Madam Helga went on. "You, the kind and helpful and understanding doctor! No, you're a cynic. A seducer, a torturer and a tormenter."

Her voice disappeared in a stifled sob.

"You shall have your will," he said in a toneless voice. "You shall have your way."

Madam Helga had her way. The new life that had started to grow in her was extinguished, but she became no happier for that, and the relationship between husband and wife became no better. On the contrary, it became so much worse that the two could circle around each other for days without exchanging a word. Madam Helga turned passionately to her music; she neglected her meals and left her husband sitting alone at table while she played tempestuously on the piano or went for a lonely walk. And one day she had her bed taken out of their marital bedroom and placed in the guest room.

Entertaining at the doctor's home was a thing of the past. Madam Helga met no one, and she pretended not to be at home when friends and acquaintances came to visit her. And the doctor devoted himself to his work and drank his drinks alone in his private snuggery beside the surgery.

But both these unhappy people derived a certain consolation in their loneliness from confiding in the silent and reliable Trine. Helga told her about her life, about her triumphs as a singer, about what the major newspapers had written of her singing and her potential, about artists and important people she knew and who had knelt at her feet and worshipped her. But then *he* came, this bear, and confused her mind and her senses and carried her off, willful as he was, brutal and self-centred. She was to be his alone. She was to fade away together with him and be buried in the ultimate darkness at the edge of the world.

"But wait," she said with a smile, while her face contracted and grew cold. "He shall see he's made a mistake."

Trine said nothing, but when she had gone to bed in the evenings she surrendered to her evil forebodings and sought to stifle them in groans and prayers.

"You look a bit pale, Trine," said the doctor one evening as he rose from his solitary dinner table. "Aren't you well? Of course you're well; you're as young and strong as a filly. But you don't really like all this with my wife and me. You don't thrive in this atmosphere, of course. Neither do I. And a nasty mess it is, too. Tell me honestly what you really think about it, Trine. You're a sensible girl."

Trine sat up straight. She gave the doctor a tempestuous look and said in a loud voice, "I think it would help if you and your wife asked Jesus Christ for guidance."

The doctor smiled. He laughed a little, just a little, as though in something approaching sadness.

"Go on, Trine," he asked her. "You are such a good and honest soul. You are healthy and kind. You'll marry a splendid husband and have eight sturdy sons whom you'll feed at your breast and who will all come to love you and cling to you even when they are grown sons and chaps with grey hair and have their own children. You'll be the central feature in their lives. Rejoice in that, Trine – life is calling you, and the world is open to you."

Trine turned away. The doctor's warm, lonely voice went right through her, and she started trembling all over.

"Trine," said the doctor, "would you just pop down into the cellar and fetch me a bottle of rum and then bring me a little warm water and a bit of sugar?"

Trine suddenly decided to take seriously a resolution she had long had. She shook her head determinedly.

"*No!*," she said. "I'm not going to fetch any bottle for you. I will never do anything that could harm you."

He glanced at her warily and in some surprise.

"You are so right, my dear," he said, getting up and going over to her.

"Trine." He placed a hand on her shoulder, and she had to bite her lips so as not to melt before him.

"If only everyone were like you," said the doctor.

But now the door burst open wide, and a laughing Madam Helga entered. She gave them both a friendly nod and contrary to her usual self she was quite calm and collected.

"Yes, why not?" she said. "That's quite probably a good solution. Let's not waste any more time."

"Helga," said the doctor, who was also still in control of himself. "Aren't you ashamed of yourself?"

"No, what do you mean?" asked his wife in the same calm voice. "There's no reason why any of us three should be ashamed. Trine and I have no unresolved problems; on the contrary, we understand each other perfectly well. And as for you –?"

"Oh, this is sheer madness," said the doctor with a

rather uncertain laugh.

"Not in the least," continued his wife. "Be reasonable about it, Oskar. You love being in this country and running around all over the place, and then you say that you don't want to live without children and that you fancy a healthy, unsophisticated woman who would devote herself to her simple, noble calling, don't you? You fancy Trine; you've said so yourself, and I well understand you, for I'm also very fond of her. All right then, have her. Because as for me, there's nothing I would rather do than regain my freedom. I must *get on*. I can't stay here. You know that, both of you. There's nothing else to talk about."

"But you are completely wrong, Madam Helga," Trine managed to pull herself together to intervene.

"Not in the least, Trine. Not in the least."

Madam Helga calmly sat down. She was dressed in a bluish lilac dress, and her full, dark red hair hung in waves down over her neck and shoulders.

"Go, Trine," said the doctor.

"Forgive me for not going straight away," said Trine. "I only wanted Madam to understand the truth."

Trine was quite calm now. She looked from one to the other and withdrew, her back straight and without hurrying. But up in her room, she broke down and threw herself on her bed, weeping bitterly.

One beautiful sunny morning in May, Helga Tulinius left the country, and that same morning Trine went home to her little village by the fjord. She had lost a great deal of weight and her face had become thin and grey, while her big eyes had acquired a stony look. She was fighting a violent battle with the sin within her and with Satan, who would grant her no peace but constantly conjured up the doctor's tall, lonely, lost figure before her eyes and robbed her of her strength so that she went around and knew no peace and lay unable to sleep night after night.

Things went gradually downhill for Doctor Tulinius. Trine was horrified and upset to hear folk talking about his drinking and the negligence that became increasingly apparent in him as time passed. A kind and honest letter from the doctor, in which he asked her to return, was left unanswered, but it cost her more effort than anyone could comprehend to resist the temptation to which she was subjected, the temptation to give in and go back.

And finally that thing happened that she had felt must come, and which she feared most of all and had prayed to God that He would not allow: the unhappy doctor's death by his own hand.

Trine went to town to attend Doctor Tulinius's funeral. Pastor Rohde, who was known as a very zealous preacher, spoke of the power of sin and spared neither the dead man nor his divorced wife, and every word he uttered fell like evil, burning embers into Trine's heart and continued to glow and to accuse her in there.

The world is evil. Sin is evil. And it *hurts*.

The Baptism

The child must be baptized and given a name. He has already been waiting far too long, inexcusably long, and now it must be done. Trine achieves it by means of urgent warnings:

"Not least in times of serious illness such as there is at present, you can risk the child going to his grave without having been baptised, so the poor little soul will be doomed to wander about homeless in utter darkness among the heathen and not have a share of the forgiveness of sins and life everlasting."

Trine goes on in a most disturbing way; she grows and becomes terrible; her eyes flash like sibylline lightning. Yes, of course, the boy must be baptized and not drift around helplessly in the unknown. The mother clutches her child with her eyes closed and her mouth opened in pain, and Trine is satisfied at the sight of her concern. She slips back into her usual everyday manner and promises to arrange all the formalities. She exudes warmth and worldly efficacy.

But then there is the question of a name. Why is he to be called Arild?[1] Where on earth has that idea come from? Who was Arild? Well, no one knows. Perhaps a heathen, perhaps an atheist or a murderer. Why not *Jacob*? At least you know who he was. Jacob was the mightiest man of all time, for he wrestled with God and forced Him to bless him.

With a rather unappreciative sideways glance at Jacob Sif, Trine adds, "But of course not everyone called Jacob is quite like that …"

---

1 Arild is in fact not a name, even though it looks like one. It refers to the phrase "fra Arilds tid" meaning "from ancient times". WGJ.

Jacob Sif breaks her off and says, "I'm perhaps not all that familiar with the Bible, Trine, but I do know that the patriarch Jacob cheated his brother Esau out of his birthright."

"He bought it," Trine corrects him. "He *bought* it. Esau sold it to him honestly and properly."

Well, a grocer can't have any serious comment to make on this. Except that buying and selling can be so many different things.

So Jacob becomes the boy's name. The strong name that will help him through all the struggles of life.

"But as far as I'm concerned," says Trine sarcastically, "once he's been baptized Jacob you can call him Arild. Or Tut or Snut or whatever you like."

The young mother gives her a wounded and worried look. "Why do you hate him, Trine?" she thinks.

And quick as lightning, Trine understands the unspoken question. Her eyes have their answer ready: "Because he's the scandalous fruit of sin and disobedience."

But at the same time there is a desperate appeal in Trine's look, a plaintive prayer to Antonia: "Forgive me, forgive me – for you're mine, aren't you, you are my daughter, my poor lost child!"

And for a moment Trine is lost in her own thoughts, and her eyes take on a distant look as she thinks of the motherless little foster child who had become the essence of her days, her joy and her sorrow and her great trial and shameful defeat. But how could it have been otherwise – with those parents and with that unparalleled burden of original sin?

But all is not yet lost. Take your time, take your time. He is patient, the Great One knocking at the door.

Trine arranges everything.

Mother Pleiades

The parish clerk suggests that in view of the sickness that is so prevalent at the moment, the cold weather and the danger of infection it would be most fitting if the baptism were to be administered in the child's home, but Trine will hear nothing of it. She is going to have the sacred vaulting in the church as a framework for this ceremony. A private baptism might at a pinch be acceptable in a case of emergency for a child born in wedlock, but one born out of wedlock? No, he must not be baptised in secret and without the ringing of bells. Besides, this child is strong, so he could easily withstand that bit of cold and the danger of infection. And when all is said and done, you must also be allowed to have a bit of confidence in your God and Creator.

Sunday evening at seven o'clock then, yes please. And it will be by candlelight and that's all the better.

So the godmothers will be Trine herself, who will hold the child, and Mrs Nillegaard, who will hold his bonnet, and Urania Mireta, who is showing a childish eagerness to be present; the child's grandfather and Ekkehart, Trine's nephew, are to be godfathers.

And so the new little life is presented for baptism, and for the first time since his birth he is taken away from her, surrendered to others, while she herself sits alone in the pew in this big room. It won't take long, and then he will be back with her, and yet it feels as though something fateful and irreversible is taking place during this first separation, as though a chasm has opened, across which there is no bridge.

The empty church is cold and dark, and the candles on the altar tremble nervously in front of the great picture of the Entombment, and white breath emerges like bars and swords from the mouths and nostrils of the little congregation.

William Heinesen

Angels sing by cradle's edge
Let them echo by the grave.
To all you bless, a crown you pledge
With them you go their souls to save.

Strangely enigmatic and disturbing words. Echo by the grave! But this is a child being baptised, not taken to a funeral, she thinks.

Now the little group starts off and walks in single file into the chancel, into the shadowy vale beneath the picture of the tomb, where the black-robed priest stands by the font. The boy whimpers and complains in Trine's arms; he becomes more and more inconsolable and rends the air with his furious shrieks.

But now Trine takes the little bonnet off his head, and the priest with his white hand makes the sign of the cross over him and dedicates him to the Crucified Christ. And through the uncontrollable torrent of angry screams from the child, Trine's triumphantly positive replies can be heard to all the strange questions the priest puts to her on his behalf. They are questions in which Satan and the tormenter Pontius Pilate, Hell and Judgement Day are conjured up in dreadful earnest, but, thank God, there is finally a reference to the resurrection of the flesh and the life everlasting. The mother clings timidly to the idea of life everlasting, that distant country where spring is eternal, where the merciful sun shines and gives warmth.

For Trine's God is dreadful, and his crucified son is appalling. With a heavy heart you come to terms with them just as millions of nervous mothers have done before you, but you can never come to love this unbearable pair of gods, the son killer and his innocent victim.

The old altarpiece, in the shadow of which stands the font, speaks in sinister language of the world to which we are dedicated by baptism. It portrays the entombment of the son of man after he has been tortured to death. The tomb is a grotto, curiously unbounded in its gushing semi-darkness, and through the low opening in the background can be seen a troubled evening landscape set against the pale apocalyptic sky where Golgotha's three empty crosses rise, skewed and imploring, as though in impotent protest.

In the foreground, inside the tomb, there stand four semi-naked men with black hair and dark, coppery faces and arms, bending over the dead body, which they are laying out on the floor of the cave – a naked man, pale and dreadful, with greenish skin blotchy like mouldy linen, and with a sweetishly pious deathly smile on his sunken lips. But at his head kneel three living and despairing women, and one of these unhappy women is his mother, the woman who gave birth to him and brought him into this world. She sits by him in the dark tomb. How dreadfully she is suffering.

And suddenly, everything becomes so sad and terrifying. Cross and thorny branches and drawn swords, every inconceivable evil, suffering and distress, pass through her mind in dark and disturbing images. The Slaughter of the Innocents, the futile screams of little boys and crazed mothers, splashes of blood on snow and dead black bodies with ravens circling over them, crushed hopes, endless wars, the merciless taunting laughter of guns, insidious poison gas, devastated cities and millions of young lives that once were healthy boys and the delight and hope of their mothers ... and, like *him*, they had all been held over a font and dedicated to the crucified Christ.

For the pale man on the cross is not merely the god of those who have been maltreated and troubled, but he is also the god worshipped by troublemakers and the tormentors of nations.

But at last the sacred ceremony is over. The struggling boy settles down in his mother's embrace; the world assumes its customary shape; the priest shakes the young mother's hand and utters a few nondescript words, and there is a bit of dried shaving foam in his raven-black whiskers. And Ekkehart's kindly eyes with their white eyelashes rest on her and pour the healing balm of peace and normality into her mind.

She receives her costly gift again; all is well, and life is rich and new and vast.

Dawn of Hearts

But this new life is under threat. Dark shadows brood over it. It is like a sunrise whose red glow cruel storm-clouds seek to strangle. The epidemic has recently spread uncontrollably; many people have been hard hit by the disease and death has carried off many, but the voracious epidemic has not yet reached its peak.

Ekkehart is seriously ill. He is hovering between life and death. As usual, it is Trine who comes with these sad tidings. She brings them late one evening, just as Antonia is about to fall asleep. So now she is wide awake and can only lie there thinking about Ekkehart.

Ekkehart is one of those beings she has always known; he appeared one day in her earliest childhood: a quiet, smiling boy with fair hair and a head that was rather too big and with close-set white eyelashes that veiled his gaze and made it impish and unfathomable.

Ekkehart's father was a fisherman who lived in a small house out near the open shore, and belonging to the house there was a steeply sloping piece of stony ground, a barn and a cow.

One day, this cow has a calf, a fair and delightful creature that can walk already, and which Ekkehart allows to drink milk from a mug. The two of them resemble each other; they have the same eyes and the same calm, humorous look. But within an amazingly short time the calf turns into a cow, while Ekkehart remains the same calf-like little boy who romps in the hay and plays down on the white sandy beach of crushed shells, catching tiny sticklebacks, which he puts down in a bowl of stagnant water. And she plays with Ekkehart, and they gather mussel shells and conches that shine like mother-of-pearl down on the beach and they make chains and garlands of daisies and sea starwort, and out on the blue water the boats skim along beneath the great shower-laden sky.

Ekkehart was a generous boy. He delighted in giving things away and inventing lovely surprises. He had nimble fingers and could use both a knife and a saw, and he sawed and carved driftwood to make lots of little houses from it, a whole town with church and shops, which he coloured with tar and green boat paint and gave to Antonia as a birthday present. It was a strange sombre, black town. She didn't like the awkward houses with the skewed windows and doors that reminded her of those she saw in bad dreams. She packed it all down in a box that she kept up in the loft.

But Ekkehart was also busy with another job of which he indicated to her that she could expect a great deal, but which it would take him a long time to finish.

"It's a doll," he couldn't resist telling her one day. "A huge doll. You've never had one like it before and you've never seen one like it. It's as big as a real child, and it's so heavy you can hardly lift it."

Finally, this doll was brought out into the open. It was a terrible disappointment. Big and heavy it certainly was, but it had only a single arm and hardly any legs at all, and its face was ugly and terrible, with blind cockleshells for eyes and a fearful shark-like mouth full of jagged teeth made of crushed shells, and the nose was nothing but two dirty holes. It had all been carved out of a tree stump that had floated ashore.

Antonia tried as best she could not to show her disappointment with this ugly and unhappy creation. She sewed clothes for it so that its worst deficiencies could be covered over and hidden. She made a wig for it out of dressed hemp. But there was no hiding the tormented and evil fish-like face with the fierce mouth of a shark. You couldn't be kind to a doll like that. It couldn't even have a nice name. It was to be called *Shameface*.

Shameface was put away on her own in a dark corner and received nothing to eat, no kind words and no bed to sleep in. The other dolls were afraid of her and cried at night because they were frightened. At last, Antonia made a firm decision. She took Shameface up into the loft and flung her over into a dark cubby hole up there.

So now Shameface lay up there freezing in the dark and grinning miserably in her isolation, like some ridiculous and ugly fish at the bottom of the sea.

But the next time she met Ekkehart and he asked her how the doll was getting on, she had to turn her back to him out of sorrow and shame.

"It's fine," she lied.

She grabbed a piece of sorrel and filled her hand with seeds, which she sprinkled around and let the wind blow away.

"Have you given her a name?" asked Ekkehart.

She quickly replied,

"Yes, she's got a lovely name, I've called her *Seagold*."

She glanced at Ekkehart and saw how kind and radiant he looked and how he stood there quite overcome by the fine name, which he repeated silently to himself.

"You're a clumsy lump, Ekkehart," she shouted through twisted lips. "You can't catch me. Just you try."

She set off to run up the stony slope, screaming and

whining when she heard he was on her heels. She leapt up on to the roof of the low barn, stood there and made faces and squinted at the sun while pointing her fingers at Ekkehart:

"See. Didn't I say so? You couldn't catch me."

"I could catch you all right if I came up on the roof," said Ekkehart.

"Yes, but you don't dare," she shrieked.

Ekkehart laughed indulgently and the next moment was up on the roof, where he sat dangling his legs over the eaves.

"Well, catch me then," she shouted.

"Well I don't need to 'cause you're caught already," he dismissed the idea and remained sitting there.

"Your doll's not called Seagold at all," she shouted. "It's only called *Shameface*."

She went up to the ridge of the roof and slid down on the other side. She ran down through the summery meadows where daisies and golden buttercups shone and sparkled in the grass. She ran down to the shore, where the thousands of seaweed tops twinkled wet in the midday sun; she ran home, up into the loft and into the pitch dark cubby hole where Ekkehart's doll had been flung. She placed the clumsy body on her knee, bent down and kissed its rough, cold cheek, and she passionately hugged the ugly head and spoke tender, tearful words to it:

"You're not going to be called Shameface, you shall be called Seagold. You shall grow up and be queen of all the fish in the sea. You shall live entirely on your own up here in the loft and you shall have the whole loft to yourself, and I'll come and visit you and give you mussels and tiny fish to eat, and I'll sing for you when it's time to go to sleep."

She carried the heavy block of wood across to the

light that came in through one of the gable windows. There were three windows of that kind sitting each in one upright wall of the loft. One of these windows overlooked Chamisso the pastry cook's garden, and the sunlight falling in through the mould-covered window was bottle green and played in thousands of tongues on the sloping wall. It was like being at the bottom of the sea. This was where Seagold was to live.

Antonia and Ekkehart both started school and were put in the same class. But right from the first, Ekkehart found it difficult to keep up; he was not in the least bookish. He had grown into a big, bony boy with lots of strength, but he had the same kindly, patient calf-like face with the veiled eyes and the unfathomable smile. The teachers treated him with sarcastic condescension, and his friends laughed at him when he was not listening and called him Calf Fish.

"You're not daft, you know, Ekkehart," said Antonia with a little sigh. "You could easily keep up if you could be bothered."

"Perhaps I could," sighed Ekkehart. "But then I'd be bored stiff."

Antonia made a few attempts to get him going. She showed him how easy it was to do arithmetic; it was no more difficult than gutting a fish: that's where the liver is – it's always there – and that's the heart and the stomach and its swimming bladder; they're always in the same place. Everything has its proper place. It's just a matter of putting them together in the right way when things go wrong."

"That's a lot of rubbish," said Ekkehart. "But otherwise thank you for your help. And now I'll show you something that'll please you."

He took her out to the cowshed; there was a tub of

water out there, and in the water there lay a baby seal. It was about the size of a babe-in-arms and had the loveliest skin and big, dark human eyes. The sight overwhelmed her; her face went all stiff, and she stood gaping with her mouth open. But then she woke from the spell, put a hand down into the water and caressed the twitching baby seal, stroked it along its smooth, warm skin and touched its coal-black flippers.

"Ekkehart," she said, giving him a quick smile. "Is it yours?"

"Yes. But you can have it if you want."

"Yes – but no. I can't take it with me."

"Well then, it can stay here even if it's yours."

She rose and suddenly looked him deep in the eye.

"But Ekkehart, doesn't it miss its mother terribly?"

He hadn't thought of that.

"And it can't stay in this tub for the rest of its life, because then it'd be miserable," she said.

"When I got it, I just thought you'd be pleased with it," he said.

"But if it can be mine to own," she said eagerly, taking hold of his sleeve, "I know what I would most like to do with it. I'd put it back in the water so it can find its way back to its mother. Don't you think that would be the right thing to do as well, Ekkehart?"

"Then we'll do that," he said.

"But it can wait till tomorrow," she said. "Then we can have it to look at today. But I want to come with you when you let it go."

The following day, Antonia and Ekkehart carried the tub with the seal pup down to the shore. It was a dark summer's afternoon with low cloud and mist. They went out to the furthermost point of a stony promontory. He lifted the dripping pup from the tub and handed it to her, and she stood for a moment fussing over it as though it were a child. It looked at her with deep, calm human eyes. It probably knew already that it was going to be given its freedom and allowed to go back to its mother.

Finally, she let it slide down into the green, darkling waters.

She stood there with her mouth open and a tender, unhappy expression in her eyes and watched it disappear, and she wrung her wet hands and interlaced fingers. But then she straightened up with a sign and looked at him with big eyes.

"Ekkehart," she said with an imploring movement of her neck and shoulders ... "Ekkehart won't you just give me a kiss?"

"Oh, don't be daft," he replied with a scornful laugh and immediately turned away.

When Ekkehart reached the age of fourteen, he left school and went off deep-sea fishing with his father.

Antonia was down on the jetty to wave goodbye to him. It was early in the spring, and it was snowing. He was wearing long sea boots, a woollen jersey and a yellow sou'wester with black ear flaps. He was almost a grown man already, she thought. He gave her a condescending smile.

She was also down on the jetty in May when the ship came back to land the spring catch. Ekkehart's face had acquired a blueberry red colour, and he had stern lines between his eyes, but he thawed out when he saw her and turned an even darker bluish red, and neither could she for her part refrain from blushing, for she felt so strangely schoolgirlish and uninteresting beside him.

The spring sun was shining, and two spring lambs were

dancing around on Ekkehart's father's green slope. Ekkehart got hold of them both and gave one to Antonia. They sat in the sweet-smelling grass, each holding a lamb. During the afternoon she came back dressed in her Sunday best. Ekkehart was still wearing his seaman's clothes and smelt of salt water and fish. She was aching to tell him that she had thought of him a lot and had so looked forward to his coming home, but instead she laughed at him and pointed to his chin, which was full of white down.

"Are you going to keep that fluff on your chin?" she asked

Ekkehart turned away angrily and blushed. The following day he had shaved, and the whole of his weather-beaten face was full of scratches and cuts, and the stern lines on his brow had become even sterner. They went out to the point where the baby seal had been returned to freedom. She wanted to tell him that she still had his doll, Seagold. She could also have told him that it was up in the green, flickering loft, surrounded by shells and scallops that she had gathered out here and taken up to it. Indeed, she could also have told him that she loved his doll and that it was no longer a doll, but a *memory*. But it was not fitting to tell a grown man all those things, for he would merely think it was a lot of childish nonsense.

Oh, if only she had dared tell him that she loved him! She loved him for his doll and for the seal pup and all his gifts, and she longed for him to clasp her to his woollen jersey and for him always to think about her and miss her dreadfully when he was away at sea.

But Ekkehart looked down at his big numb hands and sat smiling inscrutably to himself. He said nothing, and it was as though they could no longer speak to each other.

"He's not the least bit interested in me any longer," she thought in despair.

"Ho ho!" came a sound both smiling and challenging from up on the hill. "Just look at those two."

It was Ekkehart's younger brother and another boy, standing pointing to the lone couple out on the point.

"I'll teach you," threatened Ekkehart and lumbered off.

When Ekkehart returned from the summer fishing, there was no Antonia on the jetty to welcome him, and for the whole of that long winter he rarely saw anything of her.

One Sunday evening he was standing in the entrance to the dance hall and saw her dancing among some other young people on the floor. She was in a red dress and had her hair elegantly taken up. She was grown up now and presumably wasn't interested in him any more.

He drifted home along the wind-blown shore, heavy at heart. He thought of the sunny day when she was up on the roof of the barn and wanted him to catch her. And of the misty day out on the point when she had said, "Ekkehart won't you just give me a kiss?"

Ekkehart went to sea again, this time on a different ship, one that was going fishing right up by Bear Island. He went fishing every year, always on new ships, sometimes to Iceland, sometimes to Greenland, sometimes east to the White Sea. In the brief periods when he was home, he saw Antonia now and then. She was indeed still nice and friendly, but in a way that was no longer pleasurable, not even when she stroked his cheek and gave him a kind and encouraging wink. She was no longer his. She belonged to someone else. She got engaged to that talented man Napoleon. That came to nothing, but then she started going around with Peter – and where was *that* going to end?

He met her one evening outside the dance hall and plucked up courage to escort her home.

"You should keep away from Peter," he said in a dull voice, and in the despair occasioned by his jealousy he grabbed her hand and squeezed it so tight that she gave a little squeal and scolded him and flapped her squeezed hand in the air. And she gave him a friendly nudge with her elbow and said,

"Oh, you…"

And he felt it as though all his gut stiffened. She had no need to say more. The two little words and the tone in which they were said told him all. They said to him, "Don't you interfere, Ekkehart."

Then Peter disappeared and left her behind and unhappy.

And now your time has come, Ekkehart – at last, at last?

She for her part had expected the kind and dependable Ekkehart to come. From Trine's ambiguous utterances she understood that there was something brewing. Ekkehart would come. He would marry her and make do with her; he would save her and rejuvenate her, make her a child again so that she could once more become his playmate.

How difficult it would be, indeed almost insuperably difficult, to reject him and say no thank you.

She makes a plan of campaign; she invents a pack of lies:

"No, you see, Ekkehart dear, *Peter*'s going to come back. He's coming back this autumn, perhaps even in August, and then we're going to get married. I'm sorry for you,

Ekkehart, indeed I can't say how much it hurts me …"

But their meeting took a completely different turn from what she had been expecting. When she saw Ekkehart stand there wringing his blue sailor's cap, his young face brown and furrowed and his fair hair carefully plastered down with water and with a desperate hope burning in his blue, white-rimmed eyes, she broke down completely and was unable to say a word. She heard him say in a voice that simply was not his,

"For I've always been so terribly fond of you, ever since we were children."

Everything went black before her. She grasped his hands, she caressed his hair and cheek and made his face wet with her tears and kisses.

"No, Ekkehart," she whispered. "But we'll always be friends. You've always been my best friend, and I'll never have a better one."

They were alone in the living room, and they sat there throughout the afternoon. And when they finally parted, they were again both quite calm and happy, just as they had been in the past, and he left her comforted and with a new glow of hope in his heart.

Antonia finally falls asleep, but only briefly. She wakes up in great turmoil; she's been dreaming of Ekkehart, a confused dream, something about his coming to say goodbye and wanting to take the boy to sea with him. And she had screamed and been as though crazed with worry and distress.

It's impossible for her to fall asleep again, for she is troubled to the bottom of her soul. And although the moon is shining brightly, she gets up and lights the lamp.

"Ekkehart's dead," she thinks with horror.

And she takes the soundly sleeping child over into her bed and lies looking at the closed little face that is so far away.

But Ekkehart did not die. He survived his illness and quickly recovered.

And everyday life returns with all its blessings; the winter days, grey and white and crimson, are once more the setting for everyday life, and the light that dwells in them is the waking light, the teeming light from the dawn of time. Indeed, even in the desolate moonlight and the northern lights, spring lives and germinates along with the vast hope that embraces the world.

From the south-east gable window, which is the window in Antonia's and the boy's bedroom, it is possible on clear January mornings to see the sun rise from the vast ocean. It dresses the faded walls in its dark copper-coloured wall covering and turns the blotchy ceiling into a spreading map of the world. It draws the little room into its eternal world of joyous trust and the celebration of boundless hope; indeed, it elevates the insignificant and ridiculous so that even the most miserable chamber pot becomes a planetary miracle, and it endows the neighbourhood chanticleers with laudatory power and makes them proclaim the joy in life of all creation.

The little boy has the first meal of the day and lies babbling contentedly in his newly changed shawl, and his mother lies listening ecstatically to this chatter, this little indication that has not yet been put into words, but which nevertheless is full of incipient meaning and understanding.

He looks at her and recognizes her. A tiny shower of impatience crosses his features; he opens his mouth in sudden desire, but he is overcome by sleepiness and chatters on in a tiny affectionate melody that tells of great bliss.

Dance of Death

The great epidemic is at its height. Infuriated and thwarted at the empty trenches, silent mortars and vanished u-boats, death, that indolent old collector, has poisoned human breath itself so that night and annihilation and all the obscurantists and Seventh Day Adventists headed by Ankersen the savings bank manager can have the last word and be sure of victory.

Indeed, for one last time, the confrontational old lay preacher Ankersen is having a great time; he revels in the Book of Revelations, and his addresses are about angels descending from Heaven and carrying the keys of the depths, while scornful beasts rise snorting from the ocean. Trine the Eyes and Urania Mireta have been over to listen to him and are breathless with horror and sensation. It is almost like the old days, the days of the Ydun Christian Temperance Society, when they used to speak in tongues and the young missionary to the heathen, Matte-Gok, was murdered by the unbelievers.

But it is no longer the determined Ankersen of old from the unforgettable age of the temperance society's battles and victory. No, it is a white-haired, hardened Ankersen with an old man's impotent quiver in his voice as he bares his big, cruel cranial teeth.

But in the opinion of many people Ankersen is at his most dreadful in this final phase. After all, he was at one time a helpful person and a spokesman for life, whereas now there is nothing on his mind but death and damnation. No longer does he sing the optimistic song of the blind who see and the lame who dance in the meadow – no, his bony fingers now play the plaintive old melodeon to echo apocalyptic fears, while death, that hard, pale spindle-shank, that noseless, blind joker and gallant, hangs around quite unconcerned and selects his partners for the dance.

Aye, he especially picks strong young folk in their prime, newly married couples, women in confinement and young mothers. But children and old folk are also invited to the dance by the obscene white maniac; no one can feel safe; many die, and the Ydun Youth Association meeting hall has to be taken into use as a mortuary, and the funeral bells toll their tales of sorrow and suffering in the dusk-filled winter afternoons.

Nor does the blind and undifferentiating dancing master spare his own admirers and spokesmen: one fine day it was also Ankersen's turn; he fell at his post, collapsing over his lectern just as, with hand raised and arms outstretched, he stood invoking all the birds of the heavens and inviting them to the great banquet.

Oppressive days.

But in the midst of the gloom there are nevertheless a few points of light and glad tidings.

Chamisso the pastry cook has had a letter from his runaway daughter Jutta! A penitent, contrite letter from far-off America. She is alive and well, though Eggertsen has been arrested and put on trial for new acts of trickery. He is a terrible sinner, but he, too, repents, and she loves him and won't leave him and come home, but will wait for him even if it should be to the end of her days. She's living with people who understand her and are called *Millenists*. And both Eggertsen and she have gone over to Millenism and are now awaiting the millennium.

"Oh, dear God," sighs Mrs Chamisso, weeping and

quite overcome by so much love.

But the quick-tempered little pastry cook is neither impressed nor touched.

"I'll … I'll …" he threatens while jumping furiously on the spot and baring his teeth at the ceiling: "Ah – *ma andatevene di qui!*"

The news of Jutta's letter quickly spreads throughout the town.

"If only they don't send Eggertsen to the electric chair," squeaks Urania Mireta, staring out into the gathering darkness with a smile occasioned by dreams of unpleasant things.

"Ugh, surely not," says Mrs Nillegaard the midwife with a shudder.

"The electric chair's nothing compared with the punishment finally awaiting him," says Trine ponderously.

The three sibyls sit holding one of their coffee-scented meetings to discuss fate. They chat away in the anemic winter twilight. Mrs Nillegaard's pince-nez and Trine's eyes shine in the light from the open door of the stove.

Antonia comes through the room and goes into her bedroom. No thank you, she doesn't want any coffee. Contrary to custom she is feeling tired and sleepy, quite worn out.

The boy is sound asleep in his cradle. She lies down on the bed. She has a feeling of weariness and weight in her limbs, as though they had been filled with warm sand. Big radiant flakes are falling in the dusk. Through the half open door she can hear fragments of the three women's eager conversation. They are going over sombre memories and stories. Trine tells the one about *Marshman*. It's an old story from her distant native parts. Antonia knows it. It's so weird that she could scream at it.

Marshman was a drunk who broke into an attic room where a completely insane girl called Rachel was shut up. Rachel was alone at home, the others from the house all being at a wedding on a farm on the other side of the fjord. Marshman made to attack Rachel, but she was too strong for him; she strangled him with her bare hands and put his eyes out with his own knife. Then, singing loudly, she went out in the dark to put out the eyes of other people, and she managed to injure two men and a young woman with Marshman's knife before they managed to tie her down. But the most frightening thing of all was that throughout this crazy murderous expedition, she was singing the ancient penitential hymn, "Upon the Cross in mortal pain".

"Yes, just imagine," repeats Urania Mireta: "Upon the Cross in mortal pain".

"Ugh," says Mrs Nillegaard in a voice that is full of a right-thinking person's righteous abhorrence.

Why does Trine have to tell this story? And why does she sigh one of her long, thirsty sighs afterwards?

Antonia lies dozing and half dreaming. She is sitting in a boat without oars and without sails or motor, but it nevertheless makes good and regular progress and it knows where it's going. *She* doesn't know, and this worries her, but she's holding a wonderful warm, pulsating bundle to her heart, a gift that cannot be greater, for it's the gift of living life.

Antonia is ill and lies there in a painful slumber from which she occasionally has to wrest herself in order to see to the boy. But thank God, there is nothing wrong with him. The raging sickness doesn't attack infants; they are all, as it were, too small for its pincers; it overlooks them or rejects them in its arrogant voracity.

And yet it happens. The little face grows red and swollen; his crying turns into breathless gasping; fever is at work in the little body; this morning of life loses its glorious promise and assumes the heaviness and dullness of an evening. It's a long time before the doctor can find time to come, and it's becoming worse hour by hour. She hugs the poor, threatened life and feels it's already growing cool in her burning embrace.

"It's no use screaming, Antonia," she hears Trine's monitory voice as through a wall.

And then all the words she knows by heart and fears and hates: "a trial you have to undergo ... the will of God ... sure of salvation ... baptized and registered ... cleansed of original sin ... still free from sin ... suffer the little children to come unto me ...!"

"No," she cries and stifles her frantic cries in the bedclothes. "I bore him. I gave birth to him. He's mine and mine alone; no one has any right to him but me."

"The girl's dreadfully hysterical," says the doctor, preparing to give her an injection to calm her down. But she puts up a furious resistance; she's not going to be put outside it all now and dream it away and waken again to a void and the loneliness that will eat her up and make her mad. But she feels the iron grasps of the doctor and Trine and the little sting produced by the needle.

And the boy ... Where is he?

"Is he dead?" she groans, completely overwrought, after which she becomes infuriated again and tries to get out of bed. But Trine holds her back, and she collapses with a hollow, bubbling sigh.

"Jesus is with you," Trine seeks to speak to her. "You just have to surrender to him, for he is the Saviour ..."

In one single dreadful glimpse, Antonia catches

Trine's eye and is shaken with horror – like a lost wanderer struck by lightning one night in a tempestuous storm.

But then, suddenly, all is calm. There is a ringing in her ears, first quite delicate, then more powerful and violent, as though coming from millions of glass-clear waves, as though from miles of foaming sea. She is lying in a bed-like boat drifting out at sea; she is entirely alone, but feels quite safe, although the broad swell rocks the boat up and down, and although she is stiff, aches in every joint and is full of birth pains. For she is giving birth, a lonely woman giving birth on the tempestuous ocean, with the radiant light of morning shining upon her. And she hears a great heavenly voice that is really Trine's ordinary voice, speaking and reading from the Scripture's words on the last times: "And there appeared a great wonder in heaven; a woman clothed with the sun, and the moon under her feet, and upon her head a crown of twelve stars. And she being with child cried, travailing in birth, and pained to be delivered."

But suddenly the voice turns into a thin snarl; it is no longer a heavenly voice, nor is it a human voice, but the asthmatic voice of an angry monkey, the destructive delight and malicious mockery of death and the devil.

"And behold, she gave birth to a child, and this child died, and the carpenter Sinus, known as the Corpse Crower, came with this little coffin and the child was laid in the ground and given to the worms, and he was cold and thirsty, but could not cry for help, for his mouth was blocked with earth and worms …"

"No!" came the desperate cry from Antonia's bed, and she sat up and stared with wild, wide open eyes that yet saw nothing, while the mocking nasal voice continued:

"For behold, the poor little thing had no teeth with

which to bite and no claws with which to scratch, and no one who passed by and saw him paid heed to him, but prodded him and said, 'Where is your mother, you snotty infant? Has she completely forgotten you?'"

"No!" groaned Antonia in a rough, animal voice. "I'm here. His mother's here."

And with a cry she sprang out of bed and made to go through the door, out into the snow and the storm, out into the churchyard to the little grave. Trine and Urania Mireta sought to keep hold of her and force her down into the bed again, but she flailed around her with her arms and was completely beside herself; she hissed like a mad beast; indeed in her fury she was no longer a human being, but a spitting tiger robbed of her cub. And she was not fighting Trine and Urania Mireta, but Death himself; she could feel his iron grasp around her wrist and his cold teeth on her forehead; the pincer formed by his ribs bit into her breast, and the evil saws of his hip sockets cut into her side. Now it was her turn; she was to go out onto death's great dance floor, with a floor a mile wide sloping down to the chasm.

The music of doom rings out; the raised trombones blow a bitter winter's gale, and they are dancing among silent drifts of snow and snow-covered graves. Her breath freezes into icy spikes that rattle and break in the dark. She is no longer here or there, but she is everywhere; she is no longer a single person, but an entire host, a snowing multiplicity; her twitching hands and feet can be counted in thousands; her suffering is the suffering of the world's countless mothers … See how they twist and bleed to death on the dividing line between naught and all, those mighty beings that created the sun and the moon and all the glories of heaven and earth.

"I have seldom seen the like," says the doctor.

He raises his trombone and blows down on to her face so that her mouth and lungs are filled with needles that prick her and take her breath away.

Trine and Urania Mireta also make eager use of their trombones. And the dance goes on, but she hates and mocks the grinning dance partner; laughing scornfully, she points to the void in his eye sockets, to the empty darkness behind his ribcage and to the pitiful deficiencies in his empty crotch. Finally, she mocks him and flings the most humiliating nicknames in his face. Miserable bastard! Ship's rat! No-balls boaster! Virginal wimp!

Trine listened wide-eyed to this coarse language spoken in fever and thought it was about Peter the gravedigger.

"Yes, but that's all past and gone," she tries to impress on the girl. "All that matters now is Jesus, the Saviour knocking at the door, the Saviour who bears all the sins of the world. He's come now to take the burden of your sins upon himself."

Antonia had a difficult night. The Weeper and Mrs Nillegaard came to relieve Trine and Urania. The girl screamed for her child and was deeply confused.

"Oh, dear God," says Mrs Nillegaard, "I'm sure she thinks the child's dead. You'd better show the boy to her so she can see for herself..."

Mrs Nillegaard hurries into the sitting room and returns with the sleeping child.

The confused mother opens her eyes and lets out a shriek that shakes the house.

"Yes, but he's not dead," shouts Mrs Nillegaard as though she is speaking to someone deaf.

She shakes the boy to wake him up; he complains and wriggles and nestles against his mother. And Antonia's distorted face is suddenly itself again; inexpressible joy replaces her nameless torment for a moment.

"But Trine, didn't it ever strike you that that might give her comfort?" asks Mrs Nillegaard in amazement.

Trine shakes her head and gives a deep sigh. Her face is tormented and swollen and her eyes red veined. Alas, Trine, you pitiful and hapless divine executioner – your wages are due this evening, and they are sadness unto death.

For finally the unequal struggle comes to an end and the determined girl is forced to surrender.

You have struggled bravely and frantically, Antonia, but now the dance is finished. The dutiful heralds of the end, who are so calm as to be lethargic, take note of the signs from their commander and lower their trombones. For here, by the edge of the precipice, where the bottomless ocean of time bears the Milky Way and the Pleiades on the back of its immeasurable swell, irrevocable silence reigns.

You feel this breath from the sea, the fine starry salt of eternity that tightens the chest like drifting granules of ice, like acid fumes.

Then there is no more.

III

PARADISE REGAINED BUT LOST AGAIN

Ayo

Is there nothing more then?

Yes, he is still there, the boy whom you lost and who lost you. Not entirely lost, for your blood flows in his veins and your nature breathes in his person like a vague but inerasable memory of vanished hours of happiness and a boundless eagerness for what is to come.

The morning of time is full of your essence, Mother Pleiades. But for the moment the path leads through the strangest regions, where human beings do not exist, but only creatures with human features, enormous in size and not yet linked to time. They simply are *there* and have always been there. They are demons, both evil and good. We are in their power; they radiate happiness and fear; they are dreadful and wonderful and they fill our life with experience that transcends all understanding.

One of the first beings he remembers is *Ayo*.

Ayo – that is the triangular shadow that the little nightlight casts on the wall above the chest of drawers. Ayo remains quite still and is simply *there*. It has neither face nor limbs, but is a shadow with a soul. It's alive, it keeps watch; it knows something and takes part in something. It's kind. At least he wants it to be kind. And he also wants no one to come and do Ayo any harm.

Another being he calls *Tia* – a name that hurries past, and it is Tia's nature to be hurrying past. Tia is never still, but she has a mouth from which there issue sudden hurtful sounds, and Tia's eyes can be terrible.

When Tia comes and puts out the lamp with the mouth that blows, it hurts Ayo. The shadow trembles in fear as it disappears. This happens every evening. What becomes of Ayo? It's grown and become dreadfully big; indeed it has merged into the darkness. It's not gone. It's still with him. At all events, he wants it to be with him so he can surrender to it. It descends on him and wraps him in sleep and dream. It can't be caught and held on to; it can't be seen and it can't be heard. It can't be felt or tasted. It's only darkness and faithful vigil.

Yet sometimes he's afraid of Ayo and feels anything but safe.

It happens that Tia comes and takes the lamp, and then Ayo finds itself in terrible difficulties; it unfolds enormous wings, flutters noiselessly around in the room and is on the floor and the ceiling and all the walls; it doesn't want to go out, but it has to go with the light. It becomes furious and embittered. But it isn't him it's furious with, it's Tia. Then it disappears, and all that is left is tearful, salt darkness without Ayo.

He has a vague memory of once being entirely together with Ayo, held up on the wall and in unbounded warmth and affection and security looking into the flame in the lamp. But then something happened to make sure that he stayed *here* and Ayo stayed *there*. And then it happened that Ayo turned into something without arms or legs, just something alone on the wall.

Yet Ayo can assume a huge, multiform figure with an array of wings and become admirably alive, indeed excessively so, threatening and terrifying. Then the darkness is filled with sound of rush and bustle; there is a great flapping of wings; a battle is being fought out across the chasms in the dark morning of time, the bitter battle between the mighty birds Ayo and Tia.

But when Ayo is fixed there above the lamp like a tiny, insignificant, lonely shadow, he feels sorry for her. No one may come and harm her. He loves her.

He has known Ayo ever since the dawn of life. She comes from the beginning of time, from the millennia of the first couple of years. And he will never forget Ayo; she will accompany him throughout his life. She will take on ever new shapes and names corresponding to the changing times of his life.

And one day he will confirm what he has always known – that Ayo's soul was a reflection of his mother's soul. Only a poor reflection as pale as the moon, but nevertheless a precious reminder of the vanished radiance of the maternal sun.

The Black Bird

Tia, the tireless spirit of restlessness, who comes and puts out the lamp, is naturally none other than Trine the Eyes, Evil Trine with the stormy heart. She is living through troubled and burdensome days, feeling deeply wounded by the hand of wrath that struck Antonia down, and at the bottom of her heart she well knows that this is a mortal wound.

"I don't know what's wrong with Trine," squeaks Urania Mireta. "She hasn't a word for anyone. She's miserable. She goes around mumbling to herself. I'm sure she's ill. Everything's turned so dismal and depressing since Antonia died. And now we're haunted as well."

"Haunted?" says Mrs Nillegaard. "How do you mean?"

"Oh, I don't know. It's perhaps just something I'm imagining. But ... ugh!"

Urania Mireta shudders as she wrings her thin old-maidish hands.

"And then there's Jacob Sif," she whispers, looking furtively around in Mrs Nillegaard's overcrowded living room.

"What about him, Urania Mireta?"

"He's on the bottle. He goes drinking with Chamisso and the Houseman."

Mrs Nillegaard tosses her head and adjusts her pince-nez. She gives a quiet snort, and Urania Mireta opens her eyes to hear better.

"What's that you say, Mrs Nillegaard?"

"I say the silly chump. Aye, I've heard rumours."

"Yes, I've heard rumours as well. And they play

cards."

"And what about the boy?" asks Mrs Nillegaard. "He's not being neglected, I hope."

"Oh no. He's certainly not being neglected, far from it."

"We've been talking about him in the *child protection committee*," says Mrs Nillegaard.

"Well, she certainly sees to his protection," nods Urania Mireta reassuringly.

"What does she *protect* him from?" asks Mrs Nillegaard close to the deaf woman's ear.

"From all the forces of evil."

"Well, I never ..."

"I beg your pardon?"

"Remember me to Trine and tell her I'll pop in this afternoon and hear what it is she wants from me," shouts Mrs Nillegaard in conclusion, making it obvious to Trine's envoy that she is busy.

Mrs Nillegaard has not seen much of Trine the Eyes during the six months or more that have elapsed since Antonia's death. Trine has visibly altered; she has become very pale; her face has the aspect almost of yellow wax, and the two deep furrows between her dark eyebrows have become even deeper. But there is still not a trace of grey in her hair. And her eyes are the same as ever.

"You don't look well, Trine," says Mrs Nillegaard.

"Don't I? There's nothing wrong with me. But we're all getting older. Time passes quickly, and the end's approaching rapidly. Then comes eternity."

"Aye, then comes eternity," Mrs Nillegaard confirms, nervously adjusting her pince-nez. She is curious to discover what Trine wants of her.

"The child's still all right, I suppose?" she asks.

Trine nods.

"Do you want to have a look at him? He's asleep."

She opens the door to the bedroom. The boy is asleep, his cheeks rosy in his clean and neat little bed.

"Aye, he's a strong and healthy young man, thank God," says Mrs Nillegaard. "But he's not much like *her*. He's like ..."

"Ida," says Trine, piercing Mrs Nillegaard's eyes with her own. "Do you remember when Antonia was dying ... do you remember how she was screaming for her child? And you fetched the boy from the sitting room and gave him to her."

"Did I?"

Mrs Nillegaard suddenly starts trembling all over.

"I could have done that myself as well," says Trine.

"Well then, why didn't you? Or ... well, what are you really getting at, Trine?"

"I didn't do it," says Trine. "I wouldn't. I *wouldn't*."

"Well, but why not?" asks Mrs Nillegaard.

Trine makes no reply. She looks away. After a while, she asks:

"Do you think it was wrong of me, Ida? No, don't look so horrified. Come into the sitting room. Give me your honest opinion: Do you think it was very wrong?"

Mrs Nillegaard's cheeks flush scarlet, and the pince-nez trembles on her nose.

"It's not all that strange that I'm horrified," she says. "You really do appal me, Trine. And the answer to your question is *yes*! I can't give you any other answer. I can't understand how anyone could be so hard. I've thought of it since, time and time again. You know, it was a dying mother who wanted to see her child for the last time."

Mrs Nillegaard rummages in her handbag to find a handkerchief and holds it to her face for a moment.

"And she was able to do that, thank God," she adds in a tearful voice. "*I* certainly have no regrets about doing what I did."

"Yes, but don't get yourself so upset over it, Ida," says Trine. "I only asked. And now you've answered. And naturally I knew what your answer would be. And of course there's been a reason why you've avoided me ever since ... ever since that day. And perhaps you're right and I'm wrong. I've thought a lot about it ever since and taken myself to task over it."

The two women sit down each on her own side of the table. Trine sighs deeply and adds, "I was afraid, Ida. Afraid for my poor Antonia ... that she should die in sin. I wanted her at the last moment to turn right away from the world and accept the Crucified Christ and be converted to Him in the hour of her death. For Antonia was not really a proper believer. She was a child of this world throughout her life. Throughout her entire life, yes, right to the end. She never regretted anything. Rather, she showed off and boasted of her sin."

Mrs Nillegaard sits nervously fiddling with the fastener on her handbag.

"Sin and sin," she says tartly. "What is the greater sin, properly speaking, Trine: giving birth to an illegitimate child or *hating* an innocent little child? For that's what you do, Trine. You hate that boy."

Trine sits there, stern and black, staring into the air, her elbows on the table and her hands folded beneath her chin.

"You're wrong there, Ida," she says calmly. "I don't hate the child. I know I don't. But I hate sin. I hate and fear sin and the wages of sin, which are death. For we saw that, of course. It was death. And do you think I don't take myself to task and bitterly reproach myself and despair that things went the way they did? That the Devil should so take over my child's mind and darken it and that I was forced to stand powerless right to the end, although I did what I could? Don't you think it troubles me that misfortune and punishment were to be our lot, both hers and mine? Do you think that I can have a single moment of happiness and reassurance after this?"

Mrs Nillegaard turns away, thinking, "You are a bird of ill omen, Trine. You are *terrible*. It's not without reason that everyone's afraid of you and calls you Evil Trine. For *evil* you certainly are. And fundamentally, you know that yourself. That's why you're so desperate. That's why you're so lonely."

The piercing sound of a child crying suddenly issues from the next room. Mrs Nillegaard starts at this familiar sound that betokens life. But Trine calmly rises and goes into the bedroom. She returns with the child in her arms. The little boy is comforted and nestles against her.

"Oh well, Ida," she says, "I won't keep you any longer. But thank you for coming."

"Oh, that's all right."

Mrs Nillegaard gets up quickly and with a bent little finger flicks a tear from the tip of her nose. Oh, perhaps she ought to finish off by toning down her harsh words and thoughts a little. But Trine isn't one of the sort to encourage pity or to need comforting. For all her monstrous qualities, Trine is enormously strong. So strong that people always feel small in her presence, beaten, confused. And when they are allowed to go, they feel inexpressibly relieved, thankful to escape Trine's eyes ..!

But Mrs Nillegaard's wrath has not abated. Sombre passages

come to her mind from the Bible that as it were seem to suggest that this deathly pale, sombre old woman is right. Unreasonable and terrible words that eat into her like salt and acid – the words about him who had not come to bring peace, but a sword. And does it not also say somewhere that he who loves his son or daughter more than him is not worthy of him?

Yet at the same time she feels wounded in her innermost being, wounded as a mother and midwife, as a woman and as a human being, and she feels that life justifies her sense of distrust and hard feelings towards Trine, this barren, black bird of death.

Indeed, it has become biting cold in Trine's proximity. Bitter, frosty air, silence and disapproval surround this black, sorrowing bird. Urania Mireta wrings her hands and doesn't for the life of her know what to do; she feels almost as much alone as when long ago Trine came and helped her out of her misery. And old Blind Anna sighs in her everlasting darkness and goes more and more downhill. And no longer does Jacob Sif fill his little shop with cheerful sounds: he has acquired tired bags under his eyes and a generally morose atmosphere surrounds him. No longer does he make lucky-dip parcels or amusing verses. And smoke and sweet smells issue from the door of the little office, which has become a regular haunt for Chamisso and the Houseman and other thirsty souls.

And in the midst of this misery lies the motherless child, this fruit of a misunderstanding, crying his head off.

"Will you please look after the child for a moment, Urania Mireta," Trine snaps.

As for herself, she shuts herself up in her room. Not to rest and sleep so as to get away from her sorrows, but so that she can abandon herself entirely to them.

Mother Pleiades

Tia, the black bird, is terrible in her lonely and pointless brooding.

The House between Heaven and Hell

The dawn of time still spreads its radiance over the world, and the law of growth and renewal is irrepressibly fulfilled.

Jacob Sif's house on Watchman Hill has grown into a vast castle. Not in the sense that the business has expanded and the little grocer has become a rich and powerful man; on the contrary, his modest business is rapidly going the opposite way. The dimensions assumed by the old house are not of a palpable, but of a mythological kind, and they are due to the questing, creative spirit, the striving little figure who during these years is tirelessly seeking to make his way through the formless primal darkness of time and to the best of his ability to give things form, meaning and name.

A vast process! It has already gone on over the centuries, while epoch-making conquests have been achieved.

In the beginning, the world was a bed, a warm, damp nest in a clouded chaos. Then the happy shape of the room emerged with the lovely square of the window and the sparkling, waving light on ceiling and walls. But since then, the simple world of this room has been given new dimensions and transformed into the miracle of several rooms that is called the house, and which is full of entrances and exits, rooms and halls, nooks and crannies, dizzying staircase voids, chasms upstairs and downstairs, inside and outside.

And there are *creatures* everywhere, good and bad, peaceful and troubling. Some of them are old acquaintances like Ayo and Tia or like Grandfather. Other primal manifestations are

Mother Pleiades

Urania Mireta and Blind Anna. But new beings are constantly appearing, sometimes quite palpable creatures, sometimes dream-like personifications which he inspirits with breath and reality, and then there are sometimes beings that are half real and half mere visions.

Blind Anna is one of the latter. She can't see; her eyes are always asleep, but then all the stronger and more penetrating is the smell of smoke from her brown shawl and the sound of her deep old woman's voice.

She has her place in the corner of the kitchen by the fire, and when she has settled down there, everything changes, for the dark corner turns into the entrance to a cave, and she lives in this cave and goes in and out of it. She totters out of the darkness, enveloped in her shawl, and in a calm voice tells about what she has seen and experienced in there.

Blind Anna's deep voice is replete with darkness and familiar with everything that takes place in the darkness. No evil has any effect on her, and she fears nothing in this world. And Urania Mireta puts her ear close to her lips and opens her eyes wide as she listens, for she would like to know what there is in the cave, although she doesn't dare go in there herself.

Oohh – it's a windy day, with lots of cold and light that make your eyes smart.

The wind whistles in the chink in the door, and the rain blows in, the door blows open and in comes the *Wind* – a huge, skewiff figure, cross-eyed and with protruding teeth, the horror of horrors.

It takes him up in its long arms and dances around with him in dainty steps, and it's no use his screaming, for he is in the Wind's power, and Tia comes and speaks gently to the

Wind and calls it *Rita*.

And Tia disappears and he is alone with Rita, and after this he's often alone with this wind demon – the carpenter Sinus's lanky daughter, who comes and looks after the boy in Trine's absence.

Rita kisses him and hugs him and speaks to him in kind, consolatory words, and her voice is young and warm and makes him settle down and lose himself in listening and remembering. But it's a long time before he grows accustomed to this wind mother; she often comes to him in his dreams and blows into his mouth so that he almost loses his breath. She lives in the wind that howls outside. She's absorbed into the company of his semi-demons.

But as time passes, he comes rather to like Rita. She has something in common with Ayo. One evening when Tia is out, Rita comes and sings for him in her warm voice. And Ayo sits on the wall listening. And outside the wind howls and weeps and seeks to tempt Rita to go outside. But she stays with him and with Ayo.

They live up in the attic.

They are always there, and they dance across the floor on light feet; they chirrup and make joyful noises and shriek wildly or fearfully and hide in dark corners. They don't only stay in the attic, but they stray all over the house and are at play everywhere, even far inside Blind Anna's cave. But then they rush out again and laugh and sing in the light of day.

They regularly come to him in his dreams: small creatures, light and agile, who undress and dress at a furious pace and rush across the floor and up walls and ceilings and through the air and in and out through the flames burning in lamps and stoves. They are given various names until Blind

Anna one day tells him about *wights* – and then he knows they are wights, so that's what they are called.

The wights are unruly and fond of teasing; they are not entirely harmless, but there is someone who can keep them in check, and that's *Senia*, who lives up in the attic.

Senia, or the spinster, as she is also called, is thin and dresses in black. She often sighs and sits down with her hand under her chin and stares at him just as Tia does. He was afraid of her at first, but those days are long past.

Miss Eugenia Lindenskov is a piano teacher, and in her little room up in the attic there is a square piano covered with statuettes and vases and framed photographs. In Senia's bright little sitting room there is a delicate scent of acacia leaves and hyacinths. There are so many strange and intricate things there that they quite take your breath away, and there in the midst of all the confusion sits the big parrot, *Professor Ra*, to whom Senia talks and who answers her in her own language. Senia and Ra both talk some bird language, full of peculiar and beautiful sounds. She holds a great flesh-coloured shell to the boy's ear, and see, there's a rushing sound as though from distant hidden rooms and halls, a fascinating whispering and calling: Here, here! Are you coming soon? Are you coming?

And Senia sits down at the piano and calls to all her wights. And Professor Ra gives him a replete and condescending look. And all around him, on all the walls, there are faces and eyes that stare at him; indeed even the long feathers in the vase on the chest of drawers have big eyes that look at him all the time.

Miss Senia is sometimes overcome by an urge to hug him, which she does to the accompaniment of protracted nasal sighs. But it doesn't last long and it's nothing to be afraid of. And there's something of the same about Senia as there is with

Rita and Ayo, something rather pathetic, something to make him feel sorry for them. And yet he has a happy sense of release every time he can escape once more from Senia's room with its overpowering array of flowers and get away from Professor Ra and all those things and eyes.

But he never quite gets away from these eyes or the parrot or the long, staring peacock feathers in the vase. They all come back to him in his dreams; they establish themselves there and generate a monstrous recreation of the world in the attic's tiny universe. It's a bright and fascinating world, but it also contains some choice terrors. The staring eyes become threatening; the teeming wights are not only nice, but also a little frightening, and the parrot gradually turns into a demon of an extremely distressing kind.

This happened after he had seen a picture of a man with a bird's face, an Egyptian god, in one of Senia's many picture books. From then on, Professor Ra became a human being with a bird's face, a curiously long-legged and dressed-up chatterbox who under a mask of tortuous kindness is on the look-out for an opportunity to peck at his head.

It is blowing such a gale that the house shakes and there are wet cakes of snow sliding down all the windows. The fire rages in the stove and talks in harmony with the storm. Singing and strange hoarse cries rise from the depths of the staircase.

"We can't send him out again in this weather," he hears his grandfather say. "He's a human being after all."

Shortly afterwards, his grandfather appears in the kitchen doorway together with the person in question. And Tia takes a broom and then a brush, and she knocks and sweeps and brushes snow and mud from this man's body and feet. Her eyes radiate fury. The man is settled in the corner by the stove.

He sits there and laughs and shivers in his shaggy jersey. And suddenly he starts to sing:

> This evening, my ladies, we'll drink of the beer
> At daylight tomorrow we'll sail in good cheer.

This man is called *Jonah*. His face is a curious tulip red and just as shaggy as his jersey. His hands are enormous and hairy like mittens. He doesn't speak like other people, he just sings and laughs. He hardly has any eyes, but he has a big nose that hangs down humorously over his mouth and almost reaches his big lower lip. He doesn't want any coffee or food, he just wants to sit and sing and sing and drink from a clear little bottle he has in his hip pocket and which he takes out when Tia turns the other way. He is dirty and wet, but he is quite mad and crazy with delight.

Jonah from the Whale's Belly is grandfather's name for him. For Jonah has been swallowed by a whale and been in its stomach, but now it has spat him out on dry land, and that's why he's so happy and crazy.

In time, Jonah is taken up to the loft, where he settles down on a mattress under two old blankets.

The following morning, there is no Jonah in the loft. He has gone. But at night, when it is blowing a gale, he can still be heard singing and chanting. He laughs loud enough to shake the whole house; he is the roguish son of the storm, he dances and hoots alone and exuberantly upstairs in the dark, enormously glad to have been expelled from the belly of the whale.

The *drying loft* was generally a strange place, a luxuriant continent never entirely explored, a forgotten and secret

Trans-Himalaya. Here was the towering, vertiginous edge of the world. Here was the window from which nothing could be seen except light and darkness, the sun, the moon and the stars.

In addition to this dormer window, there were three small windows in the gable end. They were positioned upright right down by the floor, for up here everything was so delightfully skewed and happily off-centre. From these windows you could, as you wished, look out across the sea to the south or stare in at the tracts of heather and the mountainous world to the north. Or from the western window you could abandon yourself to the sight of something flickering like a thousand tongues in the sunlight, something that filled his mind with a confusion of pleasurable thoughts.

This west-facing wing of the loft, he called *Kie*. Kie is a secret green grotto, full of shimmering, scurrying life, a shallow, light-filled seabed, the home of veiled bliss. Up here in Kie lives *Gol* who has white eyes and a long mouth with lots of teeth. Gol is the guardian of Kie. Gol sits quite still up here in the green light. Gol is nice and kind like Ayo, a faithful figure with whom he is friends and for whom he feels a little sorry.

But there's no window in the east-facing wing of the loft. It's always night in there, and no one goes there except the chimney sweep and the Houseman.

This place, where it's always night, is called *Fasa-Asa*.

"Just you come in and see what it looks like," says the kindly Houseman. "There's nothing to be frightened of in here. There are just a few nice little spiders."

The Houseman lights a candle and then his pipe at the same time. And then he lies down on his back and arranges himself beneath the sloping wall, which he starts knocking with a hammer. Grandfather comes and exchanges a few words with him; they both puff away at their pipes and fill the everlasting night of Fasa-Asa with their nice clouds of smoke, and their big hands and pointing fingers make shadows on the wall. But the candle can't quite reach into the deepest part of Fasa-Asa. And right in there in the dark he imagines there's a secret stairway, an ever-so-long staircase that leads down into Blind Anna's cave and then on through the house to the cellar.

On this staircase and in the passages and crannies to which it leads down, a compelling, shady life is lived, into which which Blind Anna's songs and stories and Grandfather's nonsense verses give some sort of insight, but always only half an insight, just hints, for these are things about which you can only whisper and sing; you can't talk about them. Here live *Fingel* and *Fangel*, the Old Hag and the Sea Beast and *Creaker Who Walks on the Floor*, and here, too, there are the wights that turn up all over the place, and then there's the parrot man Professor Ra on the lookout, smiling slyly with his bent beak, splendidly dressed and with a hat and walking stick.

All these demons visit him regularly in his dreams, and most of them were neither much worse nor better than Blind Anna or Jonah or the wind girl Rita. They could be nice and kind, and then he didn't much mind if they hugged him and were affectionate. He even felt sorry for some of them and he couldn't help liking them, for instance Creaker Who Walks on the Floor. He could hear him walking about on the floor while it was dark at night. He was a sad, lonely creature, doomed always to walk the floor in darkness, and he was afraid and wanted to be freed from his captivity, but the hour of freedom never struck for poor Creaker. He was never to see the window in the roof or the other bright windows, and never was he to rest in the glories of Kie.

In addition to the secret dream staircase, there is also the real one that leads down into Grandfather's world. This world consists of the shop and the intriguing place he calls *Moke*. In Moke there is often a great deal of smoke, but this smoke isn't peat smoke or the reek from cooking in the kitchen, but tobacco smoke, blue and lingering, sweet and stinging. And here there's a paraffin stove on which you can fry apples, and a lumpy old oilcloth-covered sofa and a little stained table full of white rings and marks. Moke is Grandfather's Kie. This is where you can find him, and this is where he has visits from his two friends, Chamisso and the Houseman. The Houseman has got his name because he lays linoleum on people's floors and does other small indoor jobs. He's very thin, and his beard and hair stick out like a lamp brush. The three friends play cards on the tiny stained table.

In the evening, when the lamp is lit, the smoke takes on a reddish colour, and when the door to the cold shop is left ajar, the smoke spirits pour out into the dark and look for something out there. The moon shines in through the shop windows one evening, and now you can see the smoke spirits with their long arms and their blurred ghostly faces. They are up to something with the moon; they reach out their fingers as though to caress it and they move about quietly on the light from it as if pining for something. They belong to the moon, they are moon children.

New demons appear as time passes, and the dubious world opens further down into the depths. Hitherto undiscovered doors are opened, and new stairs lead down to worlds beneath the earthen floor of the cellar, down where *Hell* is.

And out of Hell come demons that are not to be taken lightly and will never relent. This is where the Children of Sin dwell, and the Prince of Darkness and his brood, the torturer Pontius Pilate and the traitor Judas Iscariot. When faced with these determined, evil persecutors, you stand defenceless and need help from God and Jesus, though they can both be pretty difficult, especially God. And Jesus is frightening as well when he tells you to follow him through suffering and blood and to share his torture and stand beneath the cross on which he hangs bleeding while evil men stick spears into his side and give him vinegar to drink.

Such is the terroristic image that Tia does her very best to instil in him. Trine the Eyes, of course, is doing no more than what she considers to be her onerous duty, for this infant must naturally be told the bitter truths of life and death so that he can participate in the grace that comes of faith and receive strength to undergo the trials to come. And this curiously withdrawn and nervous boy, this spineless lad, this offspring of the unfortunate Antonia, has now at last reached a level of understanding where it's possible to start purging his little soul, in the confused darkness of which the baptismal covenant fights its fight with human nature and the ponderous legacy of sin.

And gradually, his innocent heathen world dissolves. The old demons, which could be dreadful enough, but which were also touching, charming and amusing, are gradually replaced by new ones that are far more dangerous and serious.

Trembling and weeping, he has to reveal the gods of his dreams in order to have them condemned by Trine.

"May Jesus have mercy on us," she says, shaking her head. "Whatever dreadful superstition is it that's got hold of you now, child?"

And Trine mucks out the world of his dreams. She

derides his idols and overturns them with a heavy hand. What on earth are these wights and lunarians and Gol and Creaker Who Walks on the Floor and the bird man Ra – what are they all but disguised demons or at best stuff and nonsense that has to be got rid of and forgotten, and the sooner the better?

She embarks on a dreadful hunt that sickens and upsets him and indeed fills him with loathing for the ever watchful Tia, who refuses to spare even one of his secret friends.

But yes, there is a single one who finds favour with Tia, and that is Jonah.

Jonah is real enough, she admits. He was a man of God, and the whale that swallowed him was sent to him by God when Jonah was out at sea and about to drown.

Hurrah for Jonah; nothing can hurt him. See him coming with his tulip-blue nose. His eyes are overflowing with fun and kindness, and he sings and chants in a voice that almost drowns in waves of unending delight. Whooping with joy and indomitable, he breaks through the darkness, riding astride the back of the snorting whale.

During these years, however, the world house undergoes a thorough and painful transformation. The great, windy, star-twinkling void up above the roof is turned into a huge new loft that is called the House of God and where everything is strictly and solemnly arranged and guarded by cherubs with flaming swords. And the secret dark staircase turns into the way down into Purgatory, where souls are imprisoned and move about slowly in the darkness, palely illuminated from above as though by a cloud-covered moon, so that you can just sense their uneasy outline and troubled looks through the semi-darkness.

But further down still, there is a huge room with a low

ceiling, a room in which it is warm and light, and where there is a certain noise and jollity, though scarcely of a good kind. This is the Place of Torment. This is where the torturer Pontius Pilate and his terrible friend Judas and their devils go around with their strange tongs and pincers and instruments, and here are the great ovens in which the fire is never extinguished and in which sinners burn to all eternity.

Trine is not keen on talking about this place. But Urania Mireta knows everything about Hell, almost as though she herself had been down there and seen it all with her own eyes. She smiles when most keenly sensing the horror, closes her eyes to imagine it all and allows it to run cold down her spine.

It happens in his dreams that he stumbles down into this underworld by mistake. This is due to some absurd misunderstanding, and they seem to realise that down there, for the devils do him no harm. They hardly take any notice of him, concerned as they are with their hard and everlasting work, and he makes himself as little and unnoticeable as possible while hurrying across the immense floor, pretending he is looking for something he has dropped. But how is he to find the way back again? There are no doors here, and no staircases; there is nothing but the vast, hot floor.

He awakens, sweating and tearful. And Tia sighs and shakes her head admonishingly and consoles him with Jesus. But he's also afraid of this Jesus with eyes as turbulent as Tia's and with the black holes made by the nails in his hands. And he's afraid of Tia's twelve apostles, who were all crucified like Jesus, some even upside down. And he's afraid of Lazarus, of the son of the widow from Nain and daughter of the ruler of the synagogue Jairus and Tia's other invisible friends and dreadful allies from the land of the dead.

But the wind woman Rita weeps for joy at the thought of Jesus and his immeasurable goodness.

"Just think," she says dreamily, "he allowed himself to be crucified for the sakes of you and me so that we can go to Paradise and live there in everlasting joy. And he loves all children and takes them on his knee and sings for them."

Rita sings a song about Paradise, a strange, long song. He doesn't understand much of its text, but he listens fascinated to Rita's warm voice.

"Yes, that's what it's like in Paradise, where Jesus lives," she says. "And when you go to Paradise, you'll see *your mother again.*"

And in a voice carried away by longing, she tells him about his mother. She is young and beautiful; she is dressed in a raiment of bright stars, for she is a heavenly bride.

"And when you die, she will come for you and then you'll be a heavenly son, and you'll be given wings so you can fly with her wherever you like."

One night he dreams that after an endlessly long and difficult journey through the clouds he reaches the gates of Paradise. But he is not allowed to go any further, for he is not dead yet; he has to turn back and crawl all that dreadfully long way down through the vast mounds of suffocating clouds.

He wakes up, drenched in sweat. Rita is sitting by his bed, and on the wall behind the little lamp sits Ayo. He tells Rita what he has dreamt, and as she puts her lips to his burning forehead, she says in her gentle voice,

"That means you're going to die soon and go up to your mother, for you're very, very poorly. You just lie down and sleep, and Jesus will probably open the gates of Paradise for you."

And she sings to him, gently and fervently:

Mother Pleiades

E'en now I see the fruits of Paradise.
Its roses fair, its fruits entice
Me with their scents so sweet
And make my soul with joy replete.

Earth

Earth – that's the name given to the black space between Heaven and Hell, where poor human beings live in their houses and huts.

Earth is made up of dirt and dust and is a poor place in which to live; Tia and Urania Mireta, Blind Anna and Rita and everyone else all agree on this, and they talk about it and sigh their sad sighs.

On Sundays, Trine disguises herself entirely in black so that even her eyes disappear beneath her fringed scarf, and Urania Mireta is equally hymnbook black, although she has a little thing glittering at her breast, where there is also a glimpse of pale pink. Then the two earth-black old maids take the little boy's hands and go off to church to meet other Earth people all in black. All these people living in this world have sad eyes and utter sighs of longing; indeed, they would so much like to exchange their dark, sweetish smelling clothes for the pure, white raiment of bliss. They have all come from earth and dust, and at the end they will all go to their graves in the ground, but they each have an immortal soul that is visibly revealed coming out of their mouths as they sing in the cold church.

When the service comes to an end, they visit the churchyard. There are so many graves there which they must linger over and tidy up a little.

There is a soughing in the grass and the bushes and a delicate whistling of the wind in empty snail houses on the shell-strewn paths between the graves. The crosses stand in the withered grass, some of them leaning over gently as though in fond and hopeful devotion. Somewhere on one of the gravestones an open book has been carved. It's the book of death. In another place, an angel is spreading out its arms, gently calling, but its face isn't particularly nice and he doesn't feel safe with it. This is the angel of death. He's afraid it might grab his jersey and take hold of him and pull him down into the ground.

He's also scared of the little grave in which his mother is buried. She lies there waiting for him and wants to have him with her down in the ground. The hawthorn growing up around the black cross and almost hiding it whispers to him in an earnest little voice. But beneath a glass dome in the middle of the grave there is something as white as snow that he never tires of looking at.

"That's a *treasure*," says Rita. "They're holy flowers from the altar of Paradise. They'll never wither and die. They're your mother's flowers. For your mother is holy. And she can get up from her grave whenever she wants. She could be standing here with us if she wanted to. But she's invisible. But you can see her if you close your eyes."

"No, I don't want to," he says, tugging impatiently at Rita's clothes.

One day the glass dome is covered with dew, so that the treasure can't be seen.

"That's because your mother's been weeping," explains Rita.

"Why has she been weeping?"

"Because she feels sorry for all of us who've been left behind on earth and don't know the joys of Heaven."

It was indeed a pity for people on earth, for the whole of the dark and guilt-ridden generation that was tormented by illness and poverty, age and grief and fear of the damnation lurking behind death's curtain. Trine couldn't do enough to impress this on her foster-son and to give him incontrovertible evidence of it – evidence that burned itself for ever in his sensitive soul.

It was a pity for Blind Anna, who was blind and almost deaf and had lost all her seven children. It was a pity for Lukas the gravedigger's poor, snotty grandson, Young Lucas, who had only one leg and always had to hang on to a crutch, and it was even more of a pity for the Houseman's son Mathias, who was paralysed in some way and had to spend all his time either lying in his bed or propped up between pillows in a chair by the window. And there was no limit to what a pity it was for the three old Schibbye sisters, who were also helplessly bedridden and had to be fed like chickens. Trine and Urania Mireta took the boy with them to the old women's house so that he could learn a little about Earth's latest great sorrow and misery. The pale old women's faces twisted in dismay every time they were awakened once more to a life that was long since past and gone. The three bird-like creatures with their death's heads just wanted to be allowed to fly away. Tia had to shout into their ears when she read the words of the Bible to them. But they simply stared out in the air with big bloodshot eyes and understood not a word.

The living room in which the three almost centenarian sisters lay was old and low-ceilinged, and the window was half under the eaves, so it was as dark as the grave in there. Outside in the little garden there was a determined array of pale dames' violets, black-blue monkshoods and whitish green button bushes, and there were tiny wriggling loopers in the flowers' buttons.

It was awful down here among the almost dead. But

then it was more cheerful when they visited the Houseman, for there it was bright and tidy. And the Houseman's huge wife also looked really kind, but as soon as Tia started talking to her about sin and Jesus, her face took on a look of disapproval and she stared at her with tightly closed lips like someone who has an answer ready, but refrains from saying it. And the paralysed boy, who was only seven years old but could already read as well as a grown-up, looked arrogantly up from his book and said,

"You're ugly, Trine, for you've only got one eyebrow for both eyes, and that boy of yours is nasty, 'cause he's all snotty."

Trine sighed and made no reply. But later, she said to Urania Mireta, "Poor Matthias, lying there and being spoiled and now so cheeky. He's no idea that he's going to die soon. For the doctor's said that he can't live to be more than twelve years old."

"Some are sick and some are sore
And some they lie at death's dark door,"

sings the grandfather, absent-mindedly drumming his fingers on his stained trousers.

And dark winter's days pass over the Earth. And there is a despondent soughing in the dried leaves and in the withered grass on the roofs. And the smoke from all the black chimneys that stand out against the evening sky twists in silent despair. Earth is an evil and unpleasant place to be. But the twinkling stars of heaven radiate a happiness that surpasses all understanding, for they are the bright and immortal flowers of Paradise.

One evening in the midst of the darkness and gloom of winter, something quite extraordinary occurred: lights and stars were overcome by a merriment so overwhelming that the likes of it had never been seen before; the fire-breathing heavens visited the black Earth and overwhelmed it with awesome rivers of paradisiacal light.

It started with his going up into the drying loft together with Rita. It was dark in there. They sat down on the floor in front of the south-facing gable window. Something was going to happen – he didn't quite grasp what it was called, but later when he surrendered himself to the memory of it, he called it *imation*, although he was aware that this was not its proper name.

Imation starts apocalyptically in that night suddenly draws an enormous sword of light from its scabbard and cuts into strips the clouds drifting across the sky. This white wedge of light is terrifying; it comes from some spot out on the dark sea, and everything that is struck by this divine pointing finger turns as bright as day. You can see ships and boats, the ends of houses and chimneys and groups of tiny people on the jetty – all these things suddenly appear out of the darkness as though carved out of the whitest bone. For a brief second the window at which they are sitting is struck. It hurts their eyes and makes them howl, and the room in the loft is as bright as though it were bathed in morning sunlight. But then it suddenly goes dark, all at once, so it all takes your breath away.

Trembling, he clings to Rita and can feel that she, too, is shaking and trembling.

Then something terribly violent happens: an evil red Doomsday eye appears in the darkness and is followed by a blast so violent that the entire house shakes. But even before the echo of the enormous explosion has died away, a remarkable sight appears in the dark night: an island of light, a waving flowerbed of gentle, undulating blue light with manifold reflections in the waves. Then the blue light disappears, and a forest of red light is lit instead, a ferocious red gulf of light, one in which you perish; but look – out of this apocalyptic fire there grow long, curving fiery stalks that give birth to flowers of falling stars.

And coruscating spirals curl around on the spot and are lost in all-consuming smoke, and fire is poured over the earth and the sea from effervescing bowls of light.

And now it can be seen that it is all taking place on the deck of a ship.

It is only imation, a fiery game played by the ship, some great New Year entertainment played out in the darkness of night.

And with an enormous sense of delight and safety he surrenders to enjoying this show. Imation! Imation! It dazzles your eyes and you are so delighted that you are short of breath long after it's all finished.

And the imation comes back after you've gone to sleep that night; it's repeated on an even greater scale in your dreams, and now you are out in the midst of it yourself, for you are sailing on the fire-sparkling sea; you are sitting on the back of the great whale that swallowed Jonah, and you are shouting out in pure delight at the living, spinning stars. You are flying through the firmament on this fish as it hastens along. It's imation, imation. You are riding on the ecstatic heavenly fish into that vast place called *Kie* in the Milky Way, where the light ripples and rushes for miles and miles. You sail up the long track leading to the edge of the world, and far away the gates of Paradise itself stand open before you ...!

But then, suddenly, all the lights go out, and you

slowly drift down through the pitch dark firmament, deeper and deeper, and your mouth and your nose are filled with the poor, clammy earthly smell of dust and dirt, smoke and damp, sorrow and tears and the breath and bitter sighs of careworn mankind.

The Tear-Stained Rose Garden

Earth is Tia's domain, but Rita's world is Paradise. Paradise is far away, but not so far that it can't be seen when it's dark and the sky is clear, for the stars are nothing but the light from the vast, heavenly garden called Paradise.

Rita points to a group of stars:

"Just look there. Look very carefully at that patch until you can see all those little stars in it. It's a little star garden. It's your mother's garden."

"Oh," he whispers in wonderment.

"And can you see her there?"

"Yes. It's her wearing the golden crown."

"No, it's not a crown. It's a diadem. Just see how shiny it is. Seven bright stars. Seven blue jewels. 'Cause she's a heavenly bride. But the other one, the one wearing the golden crown – that's Jesus's mother, and her crown's set with all kinds of precious stones, red and blue, green and white ..."

"I can nearly see both of them quite clearly. And then I can see a man with a long stick that he's waving around and making the stars sputter."

"No," says Rita. "You think it's a big stick, but it's a big horn he's blowing, and stars come out of it, 'cause it's a *cherub* blowing the horn"

"And there and there and there and there ... There are men blowing horns everywhere, but why can't we hear them then?"

"Rubbish. We can hear them all right if only we listen properly. Listen. Can you hear now?"

"Yes." All at once, he can hear the distant heavenly horns. The air all around is filled with long, melting, ringing sounds; all that silence is one single deafening signal.

And Rita points and shows him the other little star gardens in the multitudinous paradisiacal display.

"*My* mother's got a garden as well," she says. "And my little sister and my four brothers are with her in her garden. And they miss me so, and I'm so much looking forward to going up to them and to Jesus."

Rita's mother was not really dead. She had left her husband and child many years ago and had later married a printer in Copenhagen. Rita's father, known as the *Corpse Crower*, had then married again and in his second marriage had had five children, all of whom had died in their infancy.

The Corpse Crower was an albino, with white hair and red eyes; and it was said he was not quite right in the head, but he had a loud and powerful voice and he led the hymns at every funeral. Rita's stepmother was a wizened little woman, as light as a sparrow and with eyes that were full of distant smiles as though she could always spy angels here and there and felt happily coy as a result.

The Corpse Crower and his wife lived in a tarred hut with a turf roof over by the churchyard. Between the house and the churchyard wall there was a little courtyard covered with bluish green and pale grey pebbles. It was a strange courtyard, for it was a rose garden; in the summertime it was full of red roses; they poured out from the churchyard and forced their way on ragged, thorny stalks in through the openings in the old stone wall; indeed the exuberant bush over there in the churchyard had sent runners in under the wall to produce some prickly, unruly shoots that emerged among the pebbles. There were even flowers on some of these shoots.

> Let the heart but falter and break
> My rose will me never forsake.

So sang the Corpse Crower and his wife. They sang a great deal and read aloud strange long hymns from big old hymn books. Rita's parents were profoundly religious and like Rita hoped soon to be allowed to die and be admitted to the vast rose garden in Paradise, where no sin or sorrow burdened the soul any longer, and where life was one long, blissful wedding celebration.

The scrubbed walls in Rita's parents' house were adorned with cheap oleographs of the celestial powers. God the Father was to be seen sitting in the midst of his cushions of clouds like a stern, worried old grandfather in his bed. God's Son hung here on his cross, poor and lonely, with bleeding hands and feet and a gaping sore in his side, and with the crown of thorns on his curly head. But here, too, was the picture of the Holy Mother holding the little infant Jesus in her arms. The Mother of God smiled gently and unconcernedly, and she had red rosy cheeks and shining blue eyes; on her breast she wore a sealing-wax-red carved heart, and her little boy held a little toy cross in his chubby hand.

Rita slept under the roof up in the attic. It was a little room, so low and narrow that the bed was no more than a frame on the floor itself. It resembled the wooden frames surrounding many of the graves in the churchyard. These graves were visible from Rita's tiny gable window. Pale grass roots dangled here and there from the joints in the unpainted sloping walls. It was as dark and confined as a grave in here.

But on the floor by the head of Rita's bed there was a strange treasure, a box, with a lid and sides tightly set with shells, some twisted and others small and shining like mother-of-pearl. Rita kept her jewellery and treasures in this casket.

Among them was a brooch in the shape of a red heart, and to this heart was fixed a white cross and a golden anchor. It was Faith, Hope and Charity. Then there was a red coral necklace, two gold earrings that were actually made to stick through your ear lobe and make you bleed, and finally the strangest thing of all – an eye that Rita had found down on the shore.

"It's a real human eye," she said. "It's more valuable than any precious stone, for it's the pupil of an eye."

"Just look at it," she said to him. "No, look into it properly and tell me what you can see."

There was nothing to be seen in the staring glass eye apart from a shiny dot, a tiny star.

"Take a good long look at it," Rita exhorted him. "Until you can see a *cross*."

"Yes, I can see a cross now."

"And what's on that cross?" whispered Rita. "Take a good look."

"Jesus."

"Right," said Rita, hugging him to her. "I knew you'd be able to see it. I can see it as well. But only those who are going to die and go to heaven before long can see it."

And she started telling him how they would both soon be dying and going to heaven. They lay on the floor in her little sepulchral bed, and she was staring up at the ceiling and in a quiet voice filled with longing talking about the joys of Paradise.

"See, there's your mother's rose garden. It's full of

roses that she waters with a silver can, 'cause she's a heavenly bride. But do you know what that can's filled with? It's got tears in it, not water. They're her own tears that she's cried because she misses you so."

He could see this vision so clearly that his heart beat more strongly. He could see the little silver can shining in the sun.

"And look who's coming over there where the Lamb's throne stands."

"Jesus."

"Yes, and what's Jesus dressed in?"

"Gold. No, sunshine."

"No, he's not wearing clothes at all. 'Cause they've taken his clothes and cast lots for his cloak. And he's wearing his crown of thorns on his head. And what's he holding in his hand?"

"A candlestick with seven candles."

"No, a reed."

"A reed?"

"Yes, a reed. And why is he stooping so? And why is he groaning and weeping? And what is he carrying on his shoulder?"

"The sins of the world."

"Yes. But what is it he's dragging and almost falling under because it's so heavy? Something made of wood."

"A big cross."

"Yes, and who's going to be crucified on that cross?" whispered Rita, starting to weep.

"He is."

"Why?"

He was not going to answer any more now, but was rather more interested in asking:

"What does my mother say to Jesus's mother, and what does she answer?"

"They don't speak to each other," sighed Rita. "They dance with the others around the throne of the Lamb."

Rita quietly hummed in his ear the song the two mothers were singing as, hand in hand, they danced around the Lamb's throne in the red rose garden.

> Oh come, my king, and welcome be,
> What joy and bliss you bring to me.

They could lie thus for a long time, losing themselves in paradisiacal fantasies until the boy finally fell asleep in Rita's arm with her lips against his cheek.

The roses wither. It turns cold and dark; winter returns with snow and sleet, but also with moon and stars. The angelic hosts are celebrating in Paradise, dancing with flashing lights around the throne of the Lamb.

"Just look how they sparkle," says Rita, whispering as though she were afraid of disturbing the child. "They're all shining jewels."

They are indeed jewels. Some are big and bright, constantly changing colour and beating like tiny hearts. Others are hazy, as though shining through water. Many are so tiny that it's only just possible to distinguish them. They are like pin pricks. The frozen road leading to the church sparkles with gems. And the long line of windows in the church is full of trembling lights, row upon row.

There's a wedding being celebrated in there. The vaulted space is full of trembling candles, and through all this light sail the two model ships that hang from the ceiling. The bride, dressed all in white, stands before the altar as though in a radiant mist, with flowers and stars in her hair.

Rita's eyes are sparkling, and she is so transported she can scarcely sing. She holds the boy's hand tight, and tears run down her cheeks like living gems.

Two huge candles burn on the altar beneath the dark altarpiece, and between them stands the sacred candlestick with seven candles. But through this grille of light the pale divine face of the dead man can be seen along with the human face of the holy mother, her eyes closed in sorrow.

Rita stops weeping, but she continues to clutch his hand as she abandons herself to singing the hymn in a deep, warm voice.

It is January, cold and mighty with frost and snow and long hours of dusk that imperceptibly merge into a merry moon-intoxicated darkness.

The long toboggan slope, which is otherwise left unattended, has acquired a magic life; it has suddenly become a centre of the world, milling with children of all ages, from tiny tots that have to be lifted and dragged right up to some who are almost grown up and hold forth and assert themselves shamelessly. And here are sledges of all sizes and qualities, extending all the way from big ones equipped with iron runners, sounding as threatening as men-of-war and always invincibly to be found in the front row, down to the most miserable little wagon seats manned by solitary but implacable also-rans who keep to the edges of the slide in order to save life and limb.

Cries of delight and howls of fear, cascades of laughter, oaths, the barking of dogs and implacable warnings fill the frozen twilight, and the air is replete with all kinds of smells, of clothing and hair, of orange peel, resin, whale oil, sweat and liquorice and mouldy old leather.

Rita has a good, well-maintained sledge that her father once made for her while she was a child. It's white and long and smells of fresh paint. People have respect for this long, supple sledge; it's always in the middle of the track and in the front row, and its owner refuses to take things lying down and is quick to answer back when the big boys shout shameless taunts and complaints at her.

"There she is again, the lanky lass on the coffin," come their cruel and envious shouts as she sweeps past.

Rita laughs derisively back at them:

"Get out of the way, *toolbox*!"

Rita is hardly to be recognised on the evenings of such toboggan runs. Her face is flushed and her voice is hoarse, and in child-like enthusiasm she abandons herself to the mad rush down the shining slope. The weepy dreamer from the rose garden and the tiny sepulchral chamber has been completely transformed here and turned into an imperious, roguish creature. It is as though she has imbibed some ungovernable courage from the sharp winter air. Her little companion is at once proud of her and afraid of her.

At the end of the slide there is a stony river bed, and most of the sledges stop at the edge of this river or turn aside to avoid crashing against the great masses of rock, but there is a narrow, skewed cutting between two of the biggest boulders, a dangerous path that only the bravest boys dare tackle. But with no hesitation, Rita steers her sledge through the narrow gap. Then it bounds across a tiny rise on the other side and runs on down a long slope, finally simply coming to a halt in a snowdrift.

It's all lonely and quiet here, the shouts from the toboggan slope combine to form something like a seething blend of wind and surf, and the pale twilight sky suddenly becomes so overwhelmingly close, as though you could step into it and walk on its expansive desert floor.

"Is this the edge of the world?" he asks

Rita arranges her headscarf as she looks out into the dazzlingly bright space.

"Perhaps," she says brusquely.

Then comes the slow climb back, in the course of which they look forward immensely to the next time.

One evening, Rita is suddenly tired of the toboggan slope and turns her back on it. One of the bigger boys has called her something that makes her feel sick, something she doesn't want to hear again.

"Come on," she says. "We'll go somewhere else. I know a much bigger and better slope that we can have for ourselves, 'cause they *daren't* go tobogganing there."

They set off, though not eagerly and expectantly as has otherwise been the case. Rita goes slowly, step by step, as though there were no hurry at all, and she stares thoughtfully ahead. The wind is blowing, the snow beneath their feet chatters like birds and they feel the frosty air in their nostrils like the scent of some enormous loneliness, the petrifying fragrance of nothing such as ice crystals and stars produce. The din from the toboggan slope fades into the distance and is reduced to a slight ringing in their ears. They reach the top of a ridge, where the snow blows silently around their feet and flows along like water in some great river. Now and then a gust of wind whirls the fine drifting snow into the air.

And suddenly they come to the end of the ridge and they find themselves standing on the top of a high slope that vanishes into a spreading bluish landscape where swirling clouds of blown snow come and go. And on the farthest edge of this landscape there stands a shining column spreading a powerful sheen on the snow and the sky.

"That's the edge of the world," says Rita.

She says this in such a way as though her words conveyed something inevitable and not simply pleasant, and he feels giddy at the thought of the place where everything comes to an end.

They stand for a while and stare out towards the edge of the world. Then she gets the toboggan ready.

"Come on."

"But I daren't."

"Then I'm going on my own," she says, and without further ado she has sat down on the toboggan and set off, disappearing in a swirl of drifting snow.

All that remains are two shining toboggan tracks. But now she comes into view again far below, a rapidly moving black dot that suddenly turns into two dots, both of which fly high into the air and disappear.

"Rita's dead." The terrifying thought flashes through his mind as with a thumping heart he stares down into the valley.

A new gust of wind sweeps along and for a moment envelops everything in drifting snow. Then it clears again, and a black dot appears down there once more and turns into a line and acquires arms and legs and is dragging a toboggan behind it. Rita isn't dead. She's coming back! He shouts out to her and dances for joy.

But suddenly he realises that the shining column on the edge of the world has turned into a forest of light, a living, moving forest. Tongues of light flicker across the heavens, a shimmering light just like in Kie, but terrifying in its size – a stormy, sweeping Kie on the edge of the world.

"Look," he shouts in a mixture of fear and delight. "Just look, Rita."

"Yes," she replies as, flushed and out of breath, she turns towards this vision in the sky. "Yes, just look. That's Heaven. That's the edge of the world. That's the walls of Paradise. That's Paradise, my boy; that's Paradise you can see. Look at the crowds there waving to us and calling to us. Now we're coming. Now we're coming."

And as though commanded by Rita, the heavenly tongues of fire turn into a ring wall of light, multi-coloured dancing light, and within this wall can be seen another wall of flickering light, a new wondrous Kie, and above this yet another Kie – a threefold flaming and dazzling wall around Paradise. But then these walls collapse – not with a deafening roar, but quite silently, as though it were all not really true, but only imation. They collapse and flee, but then they reappear quite suddenly in another part of the heavens, as though they were playing a wonderful prank; they turn into flickering patches of light, playfully filling the entire expanse from north to south, from east to west, like thousands of mad heavenly kisses. And at the same time a new wall emerges where the first fiery column could be seen, and it shines in deep, intoxicated colours and glitters as though made of living jewels.

"Come on," says Rita. "You've got to come with me this time."

Yes. He'll go with her this time; he's not afraid either of death or of the end of the world.

He shrieks, quite beside himself with delight, as they slide out across the top of the hillside and into the great race downhill, and now Rita also shrieks and shouts. They cry out in delight together as they rush down the hill between boulders and deep snowdrifts shimmering in the light from the edge of the world, and their howls produce a delighted and senseless echo from high above and far below.

Many days and nights pass, and many new things happen, but for a long time there is nothing that can dim the memory of the Northern Lights' heaven-embracing paradisiacal magnificence and the wild toboggan trip to the edge of the world.

How did this challenging and irresponsible death ride end? It ended miraculously in your not going to heaven at all, but coming home again, tired and hungry, sleepy and with a runny nose. But yet with a seed from the ecstatic and ferocious expanse of the heavens for ever planted in your soul, a seed of light and joy that is destined always to grow and develop there.

But now what about Rita, your childhood's bizarre and munificent giver and magician, what about her? She trod her own dark paths in unknown realms, where heaven and hell meet, a closed land known to no one but her.

"Now you shall see what it's like in Paradise," said Rita one day.

Summer had come again, and it was a mild and scented late morning with sunshine and showers.

She crept in beneath the roses hanging in the churchyard, which were full of sparkling raindrops from the last shower. She got through with difficulty and at the cost of a great struggle. The prickly branches tore at her hair and scratched her cheeks and forehead. She pulled a face and clenched her teeth, and finally she managed to make it through. She settled in the intractable, wet covering of leaves and arranged it around her shoulders and meagre breast. There were brightly-coloured roses in her hair, and the saw-toothed foliage hung down her ungainly body like a gown, a gruesome cloak. Her forehead bled a little. And now she raised her face and, with a faraway look in eyes turned to heaven, she started to sing:

> With reed of mockery in pious hands
> With thorns of pain around his head
> And stains of purple where he's bled
> My Jesus 'fore cruel Pilate stands.

"Rita," the little boy couldn't but shout out, for he was almost sure that she was going to die now.

But she was quite unconcerned as she sang her long hymn to the end. And after this she remained sitting there, quite quietly, with her head bowed and her eyes closed, as though her soul had left this world and been adopted into the host of blessed spirits.

"Rita."

She looked up and stared at him fondly and dreamily. Great tears ran down her cheeks, and two tiny droplets of blood trickled down her forehead.

Now many days pass without Rita being seen.

She has disappeared. Is she dead? No, she's not dead, and neither is she ill. She is *all peculiar*.

Gradually it emerges that Rita has become so peculiar that she can't be together with other people. But that doesn't upset her; she's happy. She sings all the time. She's forgotten everything. She's *mad*.

He never saw Rita again, but some years later he heard her singing. It was late one afternoon, and he was playing together with other children on a flowering meadow amid a host of daisies and buttercups. It was a beautiful meadow, but there was something threatening about the place, for the madhouse was out there. The madhouse was a little grey stone building with quite small barred windows high up under the eaves, like eyes spying on you. In front of the building there was an old garden with lush red currant bushes full of red berries, but no one would eat any of those berries, for they could make you mad.

"Listen. She's singing in there. That's the Corpse Crower's daughter," said the children, going closer to listen.

He certainly heard the voice singing. It went right through him, and he stole away from the other children and found himself a lonely place in the grass, where no one could see he was weeping.

The Expulsion from Paradise

Rita is gone.

But the heavenly bride, his paradisiacal mother, is still there.

From two pictures in his grandfather's photo album it's possible to see what she looks like. In one of them she is a girl of the same age as the boy himself. She has big eyes that twinkle somewhere between solemnity and smile and she is looking pensively into the distance as though, albeit with some trepidation, she is looking forward to some long journey on which she is about to embark. In the other picture, she is a grown girl like Rita, except that she is wonderfully beautiful and happy. For she lives in Paradise and has her own rose garden.

He is infinitely proud of her because she is his mother. She is strong, she has wings, and she can unfold these wings and go wherever she wants, even down to earth. She can make herself invisible and be anywhere, even in the most remarkable places where you would least expect to find her. She is in his grandfather's shop, where she has her place right at the top on one of the shelves. But when she's there, the shelf is no longer a shelf, but a cloud, and the shop with all those things in it is a bewildering profusion of all kinds of earthly things far down beneath the cloud.

And of course she's also in Kie, and when she's there, she's the *Mermaid*.

On the wall facing the counter there hangs a big picture of a mermaid sitting in the green water and playing with a golden jewel. That's her. He never tires of looking at this picture. That's his mother when she is in Kie.

His grandfather takes the cardboard advertisement down from the wall and hands it to him.

"You can have that. It's a mermaid. It's the Norwegian sardine queen."

And the boy takes the picture of the mermaid up into the drying loft. Here it stands now on the floor in Kie, beside Gol, who takes care of Kie. Gol is also going to take care of the Mermaid and keep watch over her.

It is summer; the sun is shining through the treetops in the pastry cook Chamisso's garden, and thousands of tiny living shadows dance across the floor and up and down the sloping walls like a thousand eyes, mouths and fingers. The Mermaid stands in the midst of this confusion and her face moves in a smile and in silent speech, and she plays with her golden jewel.

She sits there at night as well. She sits and listens. She gets up and changes into a shadow. She floats down the staircase, she comes in through closed doors; she enters silently and is in the bedroom.

The Mermaid is just one of her names. The Heavenly Bride is another. A third is *Isafold*. Isafold is the proud woman who sits alone in the midst of winter's desolate snow-covered wastes. There's a picture of her on his grandfather's red packets of coffee substitute. Isafold isn't frightened of anything: she rules and gives orders; she's powerful.

Cecilia is another of her many splendid names. Up in the attic there's a picture of Saint Cecilia playing a harp. She's beautiful and incredibly gentle. She plays a harp for the angels so that the whole of Paradise resounds with her music.

Grandfather remembers a song about this. It's about

playing a harp with golden strings and about glowing tongues. He's forgotten the words, but he can remember the tune and he hums it in a broken voice and with tears in the corners of his eyes.

"Aye indeed, she's playing a harp for the angels in Heaven," he says, stroking the boy's hair.

One evening, Kie is filled with tongues of flame.

It's an evening in autumn. The leaves on Chamisso's trees glow as if on fire and move gently in the wind, and some of them fall off and slowly drop down to the ground. And on Kie's walls the tongues of the sunset sway and oscillate, dancing and dancing without cease.

And he dreams that he himself is travelling through an ocean of clouds of glowing tongues. He is together with the Heavenly Bride, and they are on their way to Paradise. And she has the celestial harp with her on this glorious journey, and she plays it so that all the glowing tongues tremble and sing.

And Ayo is there like a shadow in the vast ecstatic crowd, and Rita is there, too, holding his hand, glancing at the Heavenly Bride in courteous and respectful adoration. And Creaker Who Walks on the Floor is also allowed to be there; he has finally been freed from captivity. And Blind Anna and the one-legged Little Lucas and the Houseman's paralysed son Mathias and the Schibbye sisters and all suffering people and spirits are there in the great heavenly procession, and Jonah is there, merrily riding on the back of the whale.

And far beneath them is the Kingdom of the Earth, and still further down there is Hell. But before them is the golden gate to the Northern Lights' Paradise Garden, and the Heavenly Bride makes a sign and lo: the cherubs blow their trumpets and command the gates to open.

"Rita's completely turned the boy's head," complains Trine. "She's persuaded him that his mother lives in Paradise and has turned into some sort of divine being. God help us, but he almost believes she's mightier than God himself."

"I know he talks a lot about her," says Jacob Sif with an uneasy smile. "But ... we have to hope and believe ... that she's in Heaven."

"It's one thing to hope," says Trine and then falls silent.

She takes hold of the boy and sighs as she studies him. He no longer looks all that much like his father. He has begun to resemble his mother. He has his mother's eyes, but he still has his father's mouth and chin. And he doesn't have his mother's nature: he isn't affectionate, as she was as a child. He has recently started to be stubborn and say no. And he looks down or away when she tries to talk to him.

"Your mother," she says emphatically, "your poor mother was a perfectly ordinary human being, just like you are, just like the rest of us. She was a *sinner!* Like Eve, who listened to the serpent and plucked the apple from the tree of knowledge."

Alas, it isn't easy to explain this to a five-year-old child.

"She didn't think about Jesus. Not much at least. Nowhere near enough. Do you understand? I suppose she listened when I spoke to her. But she didn't take much notice of what I said. Although I thought she did. But if she had done, things wouldn't have gone so badly for her. 'Cause they *did go badly* for her."

Tia's voice chokes, and she says no more.

The boy looks up nervously and meets her eye.

"Yes, but she's in Paradise now," he says. "She's got

her own rose garden ... she waters it with a silver watering can ..."

Trine sighs and doggedly says, "She didn't do as God commands. She didn't obey God's commandment. And she wasn't sorry for what she did. Do you understand?"

"Yes, but now she's with God in the Garden of Paradise," he repeats stubbornly though at the same time almost on the point of tears.

"No she's not!"

Trine turns away and stares ahead as she ponders on what to say next. It isn't easy. It isn't easy. Trine sighs and suffers; she knows her heavy burden, the merciless call of her life. There's another light to be put out here.

"Do you understand, my dear ..."

"No," he interrupts her. "No, no, no!"

"Hey, what's come over you?" Trine exclaims.

"No," he shouts once more before breaking down and weeping profusely as he takes flight up into the loft.

He is afraid of Tia. And he is afraid she will take her revenge and punish him for shouting and saying no. And he is afraid that God and Jesus are angry with him as well for being disobedient and sinning and shouting no, no, no.

He takes flight into the dark area of the loft, where he has never been before except in dream. He misses Rita terribly and calls to her gently and plaintively in the darkness.

But Trine finds him again. She's not angry. She's not going to talk to him and admonish him, for after all he doesn't understand the things she wants to explain to him.

"I was so terribly fond of your mother," she says. "And of course your poor mother's in heaven with our kind and merciful God. But she's only got a modest little place. A tiny, poor little place. She's sitting on a bench by the door."

William Heinesen

But later, Trine comes to take even this place by the door away
from her. It doesn't happen suddenly, but little by little. Trine
sets about things methodically. She drums it into him evening
after evening, reading to him from a little black book called
"The True Path to God", and she teaches him the catechism.
She takes his heavenly world apart bit by bit, removing from it
all the rich splendour that Rita has imparted of her warm nature
and her sweet dreams. Trine turns it instead into a Protestant
forecourt, full of biblical passages and clothes hanging out to
dry and spring cleaning and ordinariness, and in the midst of it
all Jesus' empty cross with the washing lines attached.

"Your poor mother will get into Paradise all right, but
for the moment she's standing outside, waiting along with the
host of others who are streaming up from the Realm of the
Dead."

And now, in his mind's eye, he can glimpse the poor
sinner. She's not a heavenly bride, but a disobedient, defiant
woman who plucked the apple from the tree of knowledge and
had to be turned out of the rose garden of Paradise.

He sees her standing in the midst of the host of figures
waiting there and looking longingly towards the massive
radiant cloud of Paradise. She screws up her eyes timidly in
the lightning flashes from the cherubs' flaming swords. And
the cherubs are big and black, and their deathly pale faces have
Trine's features.

And as time passes, the image of the Heavenly Bride
becomes more and more indistinct. She is no longer the holy
companion of the Mother of God and no longer does she dance
around the throne of the Lamb. No longer does she have her
own rose garden that she can water with her can of tears.
She is *gone*, like Rita. She is only a poor creature standing
and waiting outside. She is waiting outside together with

other men and women, sinners all. And it's cold in Heaven's forecourt, and there is an evil, rank smell rising from the deep, fusty cellars of the Kingdom of the Dead, where souls are kept imprisoned and move around in the darkness with nervous eyes and anxious mouths.

And winter comes, and Kie is cold and bare, and a careworn, lonely Gol stares out into the miserable, colourless everyday light. And Rita's gone and doesn't come back. And Paradise is a long way away and soon of little interest. And the Heavenly Bride isn't a heavenly bride any longer, and nor is she the Mermaid or Isafold or the harpist Cecilia. She is simply a poor creature who has been put outside and now stands and waits. She's a poor creature. She's a sinner. A human being.

She's cold as she clasps her hands together. Trustingly she raises her pale face with its patient, waiting eyes and the open, breathing mouth.

IV

PSYCHE

The Surge of Summer

Days and nights come and go, and while winter rages a new summer is conceived in the generous depths of time, and suddenly there it *is*, fully fledged, encompassing sea and land in the surge of its vast ripening process.

The grass on the salt meadows near Ekkehart's hut has acquired fluffy tops that whisper gently in the breeze, filled with sleepy conviviality. The thousands of heads nod and rock and speak in an abundance of tiny voices.

"*Ever,*" they say.

And *ever* comes the reply from the shore, in long searching sighs. The seaweed raises and sinks its array of wet tips. There is an infinitely delicate whistling in the crushed white shells on the shore. Broken shells and empty conches speak and whisper. "Whi-i-te," they say. "We are white," whisper the tiny spectres in chorus. And with slow dreamy fingers the seaweed fumbles in the recondite Kie of the sun-drenched waters.

Something drifts lethargically in. It is hardly anything at all, for it is transparent, scarcely more than water. But it is something nevertheless. It is round. It quivers and moves; it gently waves tiny threads and fibres of living glass around. There is a little colour in it, an infinitely distant and misty colour, a pleiadian light from the dawn of time.

Yes, there you come drifting along, you ancient initiate, round and eternal like the sun, though scarcely yet existing: the first sleepy eye that ever turned to the light and drank it in, though still without seeing.

Well met, you eye from the creation, you mournfully comical creature. Hail to you, forgotten little mother of the universe. Your tardy scions sigh for you in dark and immense recognition. All bear your mark in the depths of their bodies, those precious entrails in which life is lit and comes into being, a glass-clear, fertile filigree world, counting in millions and overwhelming, a watery universe, the fount of all possibilities.

Medusa is your name, an effervescent, fragile name, nothing and yet everything in the vast ocean.

Aye, such things were to be seen here near the shore one summer afternoon in the dawn of time!

Somewhere or other in the seaweed forest there is a clearing, an open space with a green sandy bottom, and tiny black fish swim around there. This is where they live, this is their little parlour, this is where they play, and you can follow their movements with adoring eyes. How new and nimble they are, these tiny budding creatures – they are like living signs of joy itself.

But down at the bottom there's something lying in wait. You can clearly see it. There it is, quite still. Its big eyes are staring. And suddenly it rises up and moves with the speed of lightning – and in a flash it's done, so quickly that it is as though nothing has happened. But nevertheless it has snatched one of the little fish and swallowed it. For a moment we saw it unfold; big spiked wings emerged from its back and breast and caught the light; a callous jaw opened, the barbed monster was in action and did its job.

It was a sea scorpion. *Sea scorpion* is its name, a name filled with terror and loathing. It lies in wait for the small fish so as to gulp them down and eat them. It lives in their green parlour, and they can never feel entirely safe from it.

And now you've seen the great glutton and eradicator, the ugly beast that keeps watch at the bottom. And one day later, you saw how vengeance struck it. It was caught by two of the boys; it bit on their hook and was brought ashore; they hooted with disgust and a lust for revenge, and one of them had two corkscrews which he screwed down into its spiky back. Then they threw it back into the water, still with the hook in its mouth, and there it twitched on the surface and suffered being steered by them like some dreadful, living boat.

But in time the boys tired of this game. They hoisted the ugly fish ashore and dashed it against the rocks, several times until it was no longer twitching.

Then it was dead. It wasn't moving any more. It bled a little, and its mouth was all torn. Nor was it so ugly any more. It was like Gol. One of the boys took it by its tail fin and tipped it into the water. There it lay now, rocking on the surface with its white belly in the air, and it was no longer a live monster, but a dead thing. A screeching gull swooped down on it and flew off with it.

The gulls snarl, and there is really no sound in nature more dreadful than the irreconcilable cries of these beautiful, spotlessly clean birds. Neither crows nor ravens reflect any mercy in their cries, but there is nevertheless a hint of reflection in their low rattle. The brief cries of the sparrow hawk are stern and merciless, though as in the cries of all birds of prey there is a certain pithy decency about them. But the cries of gulls are indecent; they are witless like sectarian hymn-singing or the dangerous threats uttered by madmen. The merciless apocalyptic din that comes from a flock of screeching gulls is not only an ordeal for the ear, but it also disturbs the soul. What does it express? Nature's bad conscience?

No, these white sea birds are not nearly so mysterious; their demented cries are only meant as a splendid description and glorification of the sea, a panegyric to the great supporter and source of sustenance.

A threat of death resides in the deep waters.

There was a time when you couldn't conceive that fish and vermin, jellyfish and mussels and sea anemones could live in water without drowning, but you capitulated to what you could see with your own eyes. Though not without a certain sense of horror and loathing. And it was with horror you saw the blue girl Martha, Ekkehart's neighbour, dive down in the voracious waves. Martha was a keen swimmer; she swam almost every day from a little inlet by the open shore, and she wasn't afraid of either surf or snow. The whole of her body was a reddish mauve colour and her skin was all nubbly so that she looked as though she had been whipped with nettles.

But one day, Martha disappeared and had drowned. They searched for her, and they dragged the water, but gone she was, and gone she remained. The current had caught her and taken her out to sea.

People talked a great deal about Martha, and they wept over her and mourned for her. But the gulls screeched and laughed and were unconcerned; indeed they abandoned themselves to crazy raucous laughter at Martha's misfortune. And the fish smiled silently with their long, cold mouths, and the vermin waved their claws and pincers and enjoyed themselves enormously down on the bottom of the sea, and the sea anemones looked on in silent and vengeful delight, and sea scorpions and sea devils distorted their mouths in mock horror and looked suspiciously at each other.

In the entire vast expanse of the ocean there were none who mourned except the seals. For seals have mournful human eyes and can sigh and groan exactly like tired, unhappy human beings.

"Besides, seals *are* human beings," says Ekkehart.

The fact is that when people drown, they presumably go to heaven like other human beings, but if they have been really evil people, they are condemned to live in the water as seals for ever.

But on Twelfth Night they are allowed to cast off their skins and they dance in the moonlight on the cliffs along the shoreline and for a time they are human beings once more.

But one day, a fisherman lay watching near the shore and saw the seals come ashore and throw off their skins and sing and dance like human beings, and one of them was a young woman, and she danced and sang more beautifully than all the others. When morning came and the seals donned their skins to return to the sea, the young seal girl's skin was gone, for the fisherman had taken it. And he forced the girl, now bereft of her seal's skin, to be his wife. And he locked the skin down in a chest, and he always kept the key to this chest with him on a ring around his neck. And they lived together for two years and had a son whose tiny feet were webbed.

One day, when he was out at sea, the fisherman suddenly turned terribly pale, for the key to the chest had gone and instead there was the thigh bone of a seabird hanging round his neck beneath his jersey. And he said to his companions, "Today I have become a widower."

And when he came home, the seal girl had gone, and there was no one in the house but his little son, who lay there well fed and warm in his cradle. But his pillow was still wet from his mother's tears. And from that time, a black seal often appeared on the coast close to the fisherman's hut, and when the boy was playing on the shore, it would come quite close and stare sadly at him.

"Were you that fisherman, Ekkehart?"

Ekkehart shook his head. He laughed sadly at the thought and at himself and at the little boy who could produce such a silly question.

"Yes, it was you, wasn't it?" the boy went on stubbornly.

"No, of course it wasn't me. How can you imagine anything as stupid as that? It's only an old legend."

"An old legend? – What's that?"

"Well, what is it? It's something that never happened, but which perhaps could have happened. Or ... no, I don't know."

Ekkehart smiles again and falls silent.

"Well, I did once have a baby seal and I gave it to your mother, but she felt sorry for it, and so we put it back in the water."

"And didn't it ever come back to you?" the boy asks eagerly.

"No."

"So is that only an old ... whatever you called it?"

"Legend. No, that's not a legend, because it really happened."

They exchanged glances. Ekkehart had to laugh to

himself again for the boy's eyes were once more full of doubt and suspicion.

"Yes, but Ekkehart, wasn't that baby seal ... wasn't it the son you were telling me about before, the one the fisherman and the seal girl had?"

Now Ekkehart really had to laugh aloud.

"Yes, it was *you* of course," he laughed. "The little baby seal was you. How could you doubt that?"

And now it's been said, and it's not much use then when Ekkehart later nudges him and tries to dismiss it all as a lot of nonsense.

And the day passes and the summer takes its long, light course and many things happen, but the most remarkable of them all continues to be this idea that he's Ekkehart and the Seal Girl's son. Even if your toes are not webbed, you can still stretch them out and make your foot look like a flipper. And if down on the beach you see a black seal lying there staring at you, then it's your mother.

And in some remarkable way it all chimes in with Trine's words: "Your mother was a sinner." For of course it's only sinful, bad people who are doomed always to live in the sea as seals.

On the other hand, it isn't an entirely pleasant thought. For suppose she wants to have you back in the sea and drown you there and change you into a baby seal?

And yet – it's all just a legend, as Ekkehart says. A *legend*. He savours the curious new word that slips between his teeth and goes out through his nose and blows around gently like the draught in Ekkehart's barn.

Legend. Legend.

Mother Pleiades

That summer Ekkehart was simply at the very centre of things, and you came to know and love this man whose nature was unswerving loyalty and generous strength – well hidden behind thick white eyelashes and further concealed in fleeting little smiles and jerks and nudges. Such was Ekkehart, this calf-like divinity in human form; his character wasn't well intentioned and didactic; he was rough and coarse in appearance; he didn't take himself seriously; he had no sense of being better than this person or that; he had no idea that he was one of the eternal ones who dwell in the beginning and always shall be, even if they apparently disappear.

Ekkehart disappeared. One fine day he was gone.

He vanished at sea together with twenty-seven other young fishermen. They sank during a violent spring gale, on their way to Iceland on the big schooner, the *Unda Maris*.

The *sea* took Ekkehart; enormous waves lifted him out of time and carried him over into eternity – aye, over into the only eternity that exists: the one that dwells in the human mind that is warm and grateful in its memories.

But that was not to happen until the following year. It is still summer, living and surging, and Ekkehart is still alive. He is at home this summer; he builds boats with his skilful hands. He takes part in all the summer's events; indeed, he is enduringly and unfailingly at the heart of it, its benevolent soul that cannot sufficiently be praised and loved. For he is a human being in all its ordinary and nameless glory.

Growth, contentment and wellbeing emanate from him – that primordial contentment that gives life a secure abode on earth.

Ekkehart's green and grassy world is surrounded by a moss-grown stone wall, and behind this enclosure there is another field enclosed in the same way, and then there is yet another field on a slope. But here the cultivated plots come to an end, and the *mountain* begins.

The mountain is full of rain. There it stands with its peak inserted into a billowing fog bank and like a huge world-calf it is suckled by the rain-udder. But it doesn't always rain like that. Occasionally, it clears up. And the mountain raises its water-sated body and looks around the wide world. Vast and compelling is the mountain when it shakes fog and damp off and raises itself up to the insatiable blue expanse of the heavens.

"Who lives up in the mountains?"

"No one. Well, sheep and hares. And birds. And right at the top on the highest peak there's the *eagle*."

Ekkehart's mother, who has long been dead and gone, could tell all about mountains, for she had grown up in a tiny village among the high fells. One of these mountains was in the middle of the sea and was an island all on its own. A man and his wife were the only people living out there. They had a little child that was still in its cradle. But an eagle lived up in the mountain. And one day when the child lay asleep in the sunshine outside the house, the eagle came and snatched it and took it up to its nest at the top of the highest mountain peak.

"And then what, Ekkehart?"

Ekkehart takes his time. It is a rainy day, and he is sitting there carving tiny men and women for the boy to play with. That's exciting to watch, but the story of the eagle up in the mountains is still more exciting.

"Well then, the father and mother went up the mountain together to get their little boy back. But when they came to the foot of the highest peak, the father threw himself down and hid his face in his arms, for no one could possibly get up to the eyrie on the dizzying height of the mountain. But the mother went on climbing, hanging on with fingers and toes and chin and teeth to the small cracks in the naked rock face. And she moved slowly up, although she lost her foothold several times and slipped back down again, but nevertheless she reached the eagle's nest at last and got her child back. And he was still alive, though he had no eyes, for the eagle had pecked them out."

"And what more?"

But there wasn't any more. It was only a legend. All legends come to an end and leave you consumed with thirst for more.

"Well, yes, really," says Ekkehart, nudging him. "The man on the island was me, and the woman was your mother, and you were the little boy the eagle took. What about the eyes, you say? Oh, we simply took a couple of fishes' eyes and put them in instead of the old ones, so you were just as good as before."

The mountains call and call, and you'll have to go up there some time. But first you have to see what it's like behind the furthermost wall right out there where the grassy world comes to an end.

The sun is shining; there is a scent of clover and cress; there are lightning flashes of white butterfly wings in the tall grass. Somewhere or other there stands a group of stringy, red flowers. Oh, these flowers are so very red; there they stand, so red amidst the greenery that you simply have to laugh or weep at them, and you have to stop for a while and stay with these flowers. They nod merrily in the sun and *want* something from you. What do they want from you? They are longing for you.

They want to share their happiness with you. They want to be more than the flowers of a fleeting summer. They want to be the soul of your soul; they want to be undying colours in a human mind.

And you let the red flowers enter into your soul for ever and you feel yourself filled with their riches.

That day he didn't manage to go further up than to the lonely little red flower grove. He sat down there and lost himself, falling blissfully asleep in the world of longing of the gently nodding columbines.

After a great struggle on another occasion he reached the furthest wall at the foot of the mountain and clambered over with wild eyes and a beating heart.

And now he was standing in the outfield, on the wild heath. Sheep were grazing here among stacks of peat and bubbling springs; here grew the dark, twisted ling, and here grew a plant of almost terrifying fragrance. It was thyme, and this was the mountain scent. Curlews struck up their intoxicatingly happy trills that sound like gushing springs in the air. This was the sound of the mountains and was both near and far and everywhere.

But suddenly, something happened. What? He didn't know and never discovered. He rushed off, back over the wall and down through the feathery grass, where he stumbled and fell and remained stretched out amid a multitude of daisies. But high above his head the massive mountain towered towards the heavens, and he felt its crushing power and flinched beneath its displeasure at its angry isolation.

One day, Ekkehart takes him by the hand, and off they go into the mountains.

They walk through the stubbly fields; they wander across cliffs and through flowering ling and off across great flat stretches of wet gravel in which their feet leave lonely tracks. They come to the first vast ledge, from which there is still a long way to the second and the third. They walk until they are hot and thirsty, and they quench their thirst at kindly springs, where the water bubbles up from cushions of moss as green as an eye can stand – a greenness quite bordering on violet. They pass trackless collections of lichen-grey stones around dark caves full of spiralling bracken.

Finally, they reach the top of the mountain. Here it's like being on an island in the air, nothing but stone and gravel and a lonely little lake.

This little lake is as it were more blue than it should be, and the tiny waves on it make a determined and almost disrespectful noise, as though they were angry at the arrival of visitors and were scolding them for all they were worth.

And up here on this stony table in the midst of the boundless heavens, Ekkehart is suddenly overcome by a wild joy; he swings the amazed boy in the air and tosses him up and takes him by the hands and swings him round so that sea and mountain and heaven and earth become one and form a dizzying ring of every kind of blue.

Ekkehart laughed loudly and noisily, and the little lake complained and shook its black-blue waves, and the boy hooted up at the heavens and drank in the enraptured transfiguration that dwells in the highest places on earth, where the world ends.

Summer surges and hurries along and is soon past. Evening has come for the red columbines: they nod farewell, farewell, and their grove becomes empty and deserted. The nights again become dark. It is the time of haymaking and awakening stars; the wind is sweet with the scent of hay; Ekkehart's moss-covered old barn is like a vast bed, full of darkness and sleep. It's good to lie in the hay here and listen to the wind howling and to allow yourself to be encapsulated in dream and legend.

Legend, the word echoes wistfully through the air. *It's only a legend.*

What is legend? It's something that both is and is not. There was a time when everything was legend, and one day it will all become legend again. There's a chest up in Ekkehart's little attic; it's no longer locked, for there's no *skin* to hide in it now. But in some distant time long ago the chest was locked, and you can probably almost remember that. And you remember the seal girl as well; you remember her hands, you remember her eyes – they were seal eyes.

Seals' eyes shine like wet stars in the water. One evening at dusk you again saw those eyes in the green watery darkness down by the shore, two stars that moved a little down in the deep waters; they came closer and you ran away, cold with fascination and fear. For you didn't want to go down in the depths to her.

You don't want to go down to her in the cold water where the vermin lives, and where evil mouths open in the darkness, ready to swallow you. But ...

"Ekkehart."

"Yes, what is it?"

Ekkehart is busy tarring a newly built boat.

"When's that night you were talking about, Ekkehart?"

"What night do you mean?" asks Ekkehart, continuing his tarring.

"You know, the night when the seals dance."

"Oh, Twelfth Night? That's a long way off, not until

Mother Pleiades

after Christmas. Why are you asking about *that*?"

"Oh, never mind," says the boy, dodging away. For when it comes to the point, he is after all embarrassed at what he wants Ekkehart to do: to steal her skin once more! For when all is said and done, it's nothing but a legend. And besides – who knows where the seal people dance? It might be here or there – or nowhere. And even if she came back, she wouldn't be happy, but she'd long to go down into the depths again, and she'd steal the key again and go off.

But, then, why does she lie down there watching so sadly and not at all happy to be in the water?

But now the summer is quite past.

It starts to pour with rain and the wind starts to blow, and one day a gale blows in from the sea and the surf plays havoc with the shore and the foam hosts invade the stubbly fields, full of anger and scorn.

Lonely Pain

The three ancient Schibbye sisters all died during the same night. They had their cellar beds exchanged for coffins and were laid to rest in the cold bosom of the earth in the profound darkness of winter. Trine and Urania Mireta accompanied them to the graveside, and they had the boy between them. It was a day in December just before Christmas; the sky was like a mouldy iron dome with scattered patches of rust, and all the old, cold faces in the cortege wore a cadaverous pale green and looked as though they had been carved out of mouldy cheese. And in a high-pitched, grating voice the Corpse Crower sang the ancient farewell to this world:

> From lying in wait on a darkening bier
> I am now laid to rest in clothing sheer
> My eyes are now glazed, my lips they are blue
> Give heed all you people whom once I knew.

Blind Anna also died that winter, and soon after that it was Trine's turn.

Trine the Eyes had been failing for some time, and her pale yellow face had become ever more emaciated. But she stayed on her feet and refused to hear of taking to her bed or sending for a doctor.

"I'm quite happy to die," she said to Mrs Nillegaard. "I'm just longing to leave this vale of tears. But if you think I'm expecting some special welcome in the beyond, you are very much mistaken. And if the Lord Jesus says the same to me as the rich man said to his slothful servant who buried his talent in the ground ..."

"Yes, but just listen to me," Mrs Nillegaard interrupted her with a shudder.

"I use your own words to condemn you, you wicked and slothful servant," Trine continued in an angry voice. "For thou knewest that I reap where I sowed not and gather where I have not strawed. And cast the unprofitable servant into outer darkness ..."

"Yes, but Trine," Mrs Nillegaard repeated, close to tears. "I really don't think there are many people who have employed their talents as dutifully as you have."

Trine's eyes were full of indignation, and her pale lips twisted with anger.

"Well in that case it should have been possible to find some or other fruit for my efforts, even if only a tiny one, don't you think? But where is the fruit that I can point to as mine, Ida? I wasn't even able to guide my own daughter's footsteps on the right path. I didn't pass that test. I had to suffer the humiliation of seeing God in his quite reasonable lack of confidence in me take her away from my sight." Mrs Nillegaard shuddered at the sight of Trine's eyes, but she could think of no reply.

"And then he subjected me to an even harder test," Trine continued in a low voice, "for then he gave me charge of this boy, this poor fruit of sin and chastisement ... And I did my best, Ida. – May Jesus Christ keep him and keep us all. After all I've tried to be good to him and guide him. But at the bottom of my heart ..."

"Well, of course you've been good to him," Mrs Nillegard interrupted her with a helpless whimper. "In general ..."

She was overwhelmed by powerful sobbing and could say no more.

Trine rose with difficulty and went across to the window. She stood for a while staring out into the clouded wintry dusk. Then she turned round and in a voice thick with torment said,

"But I couldn't really be fond of him – so may the Almighty forgive me if forgiveness is possible. You know, I always saw his father in him, my unhappy daughter's seducer and evil spirit. And I find it so difficult to forgive, Ida. I can't forgive myself either. And now things must go as best they can. It'll never be any different. I pray for mercy, I can't do more than that."

Trine spoke in a low, tearful voice. Mrs Nillegaard came across and touched her arm as she sought some word of consolation.

"But I knew someone," continued Trine. "I knew someone who was good to him and deeply fond of him, and that was poor Ekkehart, and it was my hope and my consolation that Ekkehart would look after him when I was gone. But then God's intention was different, and he took Ekkehart before me. Why, Ida? And what now?"

Trine suddenly clutched at her stomach with both hands; her mouth and eyes closed for a moment in pain; bent double, she went and sat on the edge of the bed.

"My dear Trine," said Mrs Nillegaard, going across and sitting beside her. "Can't I do something for you? Shouldn't I get hold of something to soothe the pain?"

Trine shook her head vigorously and in a hoarse, scornful voice said, "Nothing can soothe my pain."

"Well, just lie down on the bed for a while."

"No."

Trine was finding it difficult to speak.

"Leave me," she whispered, gently pushing Mrs Nillegaard's hands away. "Leave me alone. Please."

Trine the Eyes had a difficult, troubled death. She remained on her feet to the very end, groaning with pain, and would not hear of having help or consolation of any kind. She wanted to be alone and refused to tolerate the sight of anyone at all. Time after time, she turned Urania Mireta and the Weeper out of her room. Finally, the stubborn old maid locked her door and refused to open it for Mrs Nillegaard or for Jacob Sif, who had brought the doctor.

"But what about the priest, then, Trine?" asked Jacob Sif timidly through the chink in the door. "Shall I ask Pastor Moe to come and ... and ..."

"*No!*" Trine replied in a loud voice from inside the bedroom.

The house listened in anxious silence. Even down in the shop people whispered and moved quietly. Only occasionally was the heavy silence broken by a furious salvo of solid hail from the restless frosty sky where sun and showers were at odds with each other.

On the staircase outside Trine's bolted door human figures tiptoed around in the dusk like restless spirits. They threw irresolute glances at each other and exchanged whispered words of complaint with each other. From Tia's attic there came the occasional clucking sound, strangled and offended; it came from the parrot, whose cage was covered over with a blanket. The Houseman was sent for and stood there flipping a long, thin wallpaper knife, ready at the right moment to tease the bolt back on the closed door. Now Urania Mireta came and knelt at the keyhole, not out of curiosity but on the orders of Mrs Nillegaard. Trine was sitting on the edge of the bed with her head bowed and her face distorted with pain. She was furiously pressing her hands against her stomach.

"Oh no, we must do something," whispered Mrs Nillegaard. "We can't leave her sitting like that. We must get hold of the doctor again and get him in to her whether she likes it or not."

Jacob Sif obediently shuffled away to fetch the doctor for the second time.

"Oh no. I think she's dying," Urania Mireta suddenly squeaked, turning away from the keyhole in horror.

The Houseman inserted the knife determinedly in the chink, and the door opened. Trine was lying across the edge of the bed with her head back and her arms outstretched. She was dead. Her closed face radiated imperious and implacable sternness.

So Trine's eyes are now closed for ever, and a mysterious and unhappy human career is ended. For who can read your life's runes, Trine? You were throughout a symbol of struggle and contradiction.

You were zealous and pious for better or for worse – a Christian soul of the sombre kind, one of those tormenters and flagellants who have their uncomfortable stance beneath the black cross which the evil of this world has raised to kindness and fairness, and who with eyes full of tempest and incurable inner discord views the suffering of the innocent victim.

Jacob Sif had made sure of a coffin for Trine in good time. Her body was taken down into the sitting room by the Houseman, Chamisso and the Corpse Crower, and there Mrs Nillegaard and other kind women washed and dressed the dead Trine.

While this was taking place, Jacob Sif took his little

grandson by the hand and went a walk in the town together with Chamisso the pastry cook. On the square outside the new meeting house, the sectarians were holding one of their noisy evangelical meetings; they were screeching like gulls beneath the hissing gas light and singing their unrestrained hymns accompanied by the smiling Nimrod Smith on the reed organ; and Ammon Olsen, the draper, gave a soulful address on the crucified Christ, who through his innocent suffering and death had taken upon himself the burden of all sin and made things bright and pleasant for the children of men.

Chamisso gave Jacob Sif an eager nudge and said something in Italian as he pointed with his thumb up towards the gable window in the meeting hall.

"They've got a stock of Albion raincoats and rolls of material up there. In the loft of the temple itself! What do you think God says to that? *Si fanno i propri comodi in casa mia!*

Tia's Crossing

Trine the Eyes was not buried in the churchyard. She had wanted to be laid to rest in the earth of her native village. One morning when sleet was falling, her coffin was taken on board a motorboat that was moored down by the jetty, rocking and ready to go.

Aye, it was a morning of both sadness and solace when the black boat sailed out of the harbour with its flag at half mast and with Tia's draped coffin on the quarterdeck and headed off into a late shower-smothered sunrise. The many troubled matrons and maidens of this world accompanying the coffin shivered with cold, and their dark shawls and scarves fluttered in the salty blast. The boat raised its prow and cut through the dark coppery waves, and the foam shone red at its bow. For a brief moment, the sun showed its dazzling eye, but then it was shrouded again by a hail shower; yet it was not completely obliterated, but hung there like a strange giant dream moon above the darkening waters.

And this at once melancholy and comforting sun that shines to mark the departure returns frequently during the troubled winter's day and shows its conjuring face in the clouds. This is Tia's death sun. This is Tia's funeral sun.

And far out on the wild sea, Tia is now sailing in her coffin. Her face is tallow white; she is completely white and dressed in white; only her hair is black, intensely black like the hymn book beneath her chin, black, black like the inextinguishable sorrow of the Earth. And the sepulchral sun shines gloomily, and cherubs sound their trumpets, and Tia hears them; she opens her eyes as she listens; she awakens and rises from the dead, and now she sees that she is in the clouds, and far beneath her there are but foaming waters. She floats in the clouds above the great chasm of creation and, filled with amazement and terror, she sees God create heaven and earth.

Aye, you are opening your eyes wide now, Tia, for you thought that this creation was finished long ago and the entire world had congealed into some madness and evil that only the blood of the innocent could expiate. You didn't know that it is still only the dawn of time and that the creative light you can see is the radiance shining from the ever fresh sense of wonderment and unfading hope that are eternally present in the human mind.

Vigil

Evening falls, and the wind sweeps over sea and land and complains around gables and whistles in cracks and chimney pots. But Ajo is in her place by the wall, and now that Tia is no longer there to bother her, she is allowed to stay there in peace.

He lies staring at the shadow picture until his eyes are so full of sleep that everything turns misty. But every time he is about to doze off, he is wakened again by Urania Mireta who is sitting on the edge of his bed in her thick, grey nightdress, wringing her hands and not daring to settle down.

"Can you hear anything now?"

"No," he replies with a sigh, although he can naturally hear this and that. But it's only the wind. Or Miss Senia rummaging about up in the loft. Or Creaker Who Walks on the Floor.

Urania Mireta can hear something – not so much with her ears as with the whole of her body. The unrest there that fills the house stems not only from the wind. There is something knocking with cold knuckles on doors and moving restlessly along corridors and down staircases; she can feel it in her spine and in her hair and out through her arms, right out to her fingertips.

And now it's coming closer; now it's quite near ... no, it's *here*.

She gets up with a shriek as the door opens.

But the person who comes in is not Trine in her shroud, with hymnbook and horrified eyes; it is only Senia. But Senia is also very upset and afraid.

"There's no doubt about it, there's someone up in the drying loft; there's someone walking around up there," she says.

Miss Senia is also wearing a long nightdress, but it is pale green with dark red flowers and it reminds you of summer and columbines; no, most of all it reminds you of the roses in the Corpse Crower's rose garden.

"Come on, then we'll both go up and ..."

"Most certainly not," moans Urania Mireta, shrinking back. She makes herself very thin and small and presses her tightly clasped hand up under her chin.

"Well, it might be burglars," says Senia in her ear.

"And it could also be something else."

"Yes, but it might only be Jacob Sif, 'cause he's not gone to bed yet."

"No, they're all down in the shop drinking."

"Listen. There's someone coming up the stairs now," whispers Senia, clutching Urania Mireta's hand.

The two women embrace in unbridled dismay. They hear light footsteps on the stairs leading up to the loft. But then the sound disappears. All is quiet.

The two nightdresses each sit down on the edge of the bed. Urania Mireta stares straight ahead in mute surrender.

"It was always to be expected," she whines.

"What?"

"That she ... that she'd come back."

Miss Senia closes her eyes and shakes her head and makes a silent gesture as though to ward off a blow.

The boy surrenders to his drowsiness and falls into dream:

"Where are you going, my boy?" asks Urania Mireta, grabbing at him. But he dodges her and is out of the door, hurrying up the stairs to the loft, and is now horribly alone up there.

He finds the Seal Girl in Kie surrounded by a host of restlessly fluttering shadow leaves. He can see her face; he knows it from the photograph album; it's the gentle face of a child with big eyes wide with fear and looking forward to setting off on the long journey. She's no older than he himself is now; she's a child; she's lonely and pale and perhaps afraid. He feels nothing but warmth and tenderness for her.

But he must go on; he must go down the dark wing, and now he's in Fasa-Asa, the night place. He runs all the way down the secret staircase; it's pitch dark in here; Creaker is still walking on the floor, and there are still swarms of wights here. And Fingel and Fangel and Nightmare and Jonah in the Whale's Belly. They've all come back, for there's no Tia any longer. And the bird man Ra nods affectionately at him with his curved beak and wants to play with him and peck at his head. And he hurries on, down yet more stairs and in through the cave where Blind Anna lives and on down into the empty, moonlit shop where the smoke spirits play their slow games and dance and long for the moon.

On he goes, ever down, and the dark chasm of the stairs echoes with emptiness. But now he's gone too far down – warm waves come up to meet him, and he can hear the dull, merciless sounds coming from Hell's workshop, where the torturer Pontius Pilate and his meticulous and determined helpers are at work.

An iron hand grasps him from behind. He shrieks and tries to wriggle free. But it's only Urania Mireta's hand, and he's still in his bed, and Ajo is still there above the chest of drawers.

"Come on, my boy," says Urania Mireta. "We're going

up to Senia. We're going to spend the night up there with her."

He puts on trousers and jersey, and Urania Mireta wraps herself in a black shawl. But it is still a long time before they dare to go through the sitting room and up the stairs to the attic. Finally, they summon up courage, and Miss Senia grasps the lamp. Ajo moves and grows bigger and unfolds her furious wings. They go off breathlessly, and the two women sing in loud voices:

> A mighty fortress is our God,
> A bulwark never failing

Up in the attic they light two lamps and several candles; it becomes extraordinarily light and agreeable, and the shadows on the wall crowd together and multiply and have difficult disentangling themselves from each other. And the boy is given the big shell to listen to. And Senia talks to the parrot and comforts it, and they make tea. And Senia sits down at the piano and fills the little room with notes that hurry up and down, for they are not going to sleep now, but just stay awake.

And the two old dears smile and shake their heads at everything and everyone; they laugh aloud and tap each other with gentle hands and are quite giggly.

It's a crazy night indeed.

Down in the little office, Jacob Sif has taken Absalon Isaksen's ledger down and sits there reading and singing for the Houseman and Chamisso the pastry cook.

> Tonight's a night when none shall sleep
> Just bow and bend,
> So many do come a watch to keep

William Heinesen

For now I yearn to the dance to wend
Mid roses and flowers.

The Houseman knows the old song well and joins in the refrain. He has a curious musty voice that sounds as though it's coming out of confined cupboards and corners where it has modestly resided for measureless ages but now takes courage to come out and blithely rises to the occasion among flowering roses.

For tonight is a wake, an incomparable night, the likes of which have scarcely been seen in this house since the melancholy but great days of Absalon Isaksen.

The little room is in semi-darkness; the flame in the lamp is flickering and fighting a dogged battle with smoke and fumes. There are bottles and glasses on the table. The Houseman has just been up in the drying loft to fetch a fresh bottle of pale rum. And they toast each other and sing and celebrate a wake for Trine the Eyes. Chamisso contributes a song from his distant homeland, where vines and orange trees flower in the mild moonlight. The little pastry cook moves his shoulders up and down in melancholy motion, lost in memory.

And now the Houseman has to show his friends how enormously clever he is at standing on his head and walking on his hands, but each time he makes to bend down he bursts into laughter and splutters and spits out through his stiff beard and quite loses his strength and his skill. And besides, there isn't room here; he needs to go out into the shop, where there is more space.

Yet even there he can't get up on his hands, but behaves clumsily and foolishly and knocks a jug of vanilla pods down off a shelf.

Chamisso grabs a vanilla pod and with lightning speed

stuffs it into his mouth as though he is eating spaghetti, and Jacob Sif and the Houseman also indulge in vanilla and suck the juice out of the black pods and spit the fibres out again.

Then they go back into the office and pour some more into their glasses and sing and chant and are beside themselves with an extraordinary sense of happiness and freedom.

But the happiness is treacherous and strange. The Houseman throws himself down on the old lumpy oilcloth sofa from the days of Sofus Woolhand, and he doesn't get up again. There is a humming and buzzing in his ears and the sound of someone shouting angrily at him; it's his gigantic wife who wants him home, but he simply hasn't time for there is such a lot he needs to get done here. He is dragged off among table legs and chair legs and in under cupboards and beds and sloping ceilings; his broom-like beard blissfully sweeps across vast spaces of floor that smell of new linoleum.

And quite overcome, Jacob Sif bends back in his chair, making it overbalance and throw him down on the floor again. And there he remains; he can't be bothered getting up; he's so comfortable; he's slipped back out of time and down into the depths he knows so well and loves so faithfully, the chasm of imbibing mouths.

But out in the empty shop, Chamisso the pastry cook is dancing a lonely dance, a furious dance, a tarantella. He stamps on the floor with mercurial feet and snaps his fingers, clicks his tongue and battles with invisible enemies in the air.

"Go to Hell, Eggertsen you devil," he shouts in fury. "Or do you want me to break every bone in your body?"

He utters a long, tremendous whistle and staggers furiously into the office, fills his glass and empties it, snarls at the ceiling and stretches his arms up, his fingers are spread and his eyes roll and for the last time, on the point of tears and before oblivion overcomes him, he shouts,

"You sanctimonious sectarians! You accursed millenists. Go to Hell with your thousand year kingdom and your
Albion products. *Voi l'avete con me, ecco tutto!*

Up in the attic all falls silent.

Miss Senia and Urania Mireta have both fallen asleep
on Senia's bed settee. And the boy is half asleep in an armchair
with his legs resting on the piano stool.

He can't quite go to sleep. All those lights dazzle him
even when he closes his eyes, and the parrot sits staring fixedly
at him and makes a series of cutting remarks.

And he has to think of the pale, sad girl up there in
Kie and he feels dread and longing in the flickering dusk of
his loneliness and he's a poor creature like Ayo. And through
the howling of the wind and the multitude of nocturnal
whisperings, the familiar sound of Creaker Who Walks on
the Floor can still be heard. And down in her cave sits Blind
Anna, but now she is not only blind, but she is also dead and
hidden away for ever in the darkness of her cave. And in her
madhouse, Rita sits and sings, and her deserted toboggan
stands in the empty rose garden.

And out on the black ocean in the brooding fire of the
funereal sun, Tia's boat sails on with its flag at half mast.

But Ekkehart? Aye, Ekkehart – where is *he* tonight?

Again your thoughts return to the dark and desolate Kie,
where *she*'s waiting, that unforgettable woman with so many
names, the woman you are called to liberate when your time
comes, and to worship and defend. For she is the source of
all dream and the objective of all longing, the being over all
beings, the Great One, who out of the power of her innocence

and devotion created heaven and earth.

She is the soul, she is the Psyche through whose young, immortal breast the world draws breath.

And the night follows its course, great and wild and formless – an apathetic void, quite without time or soul, quite without longing or hope and quite without love. Unfeeling and pointless, it flashes past, the poor unborn creature, until *she* takes pity on it and gives it understanding of her own understanding and makes it live and grow in its moonless primal darkness.

Such is your being, Mother Pleiades!

As long as you are there, a new beginning will always be in sight, and life shall not despair and death shall not rule. And you will always be there, for you are not only one, you are a multiplicity and a generality.

Morning approaches. The parrot bends its head back a little and opens its beak in a tiny waning chuckle. And finally the boy, too, falls asleep in his chair and wanders through brightly lit halls, so dazzling that it hurts his eyes, and so filled with the rushing sound from a shell that it hurts his ears.

"Here. Here," comes the shout as from all the foaming seas in the world, as from the inexhaustible deep where dwell all summers and winters.

He has come into Senia's giant shell. He goes beneath sweeping ceilings of mother-of-pearl radiant with all the colours of the rainbow. And hello – he is suddenly not alone, for the bird man Professor Ra struts in, elegantly dressed and equipped with walking stick and hat, immensely kind and with feigned affectionate eyes that are secretly thinking about pecking at his head. Good morning, smiles the bent beak as it makes a benevolent approach.

William Heinesen

And he wakes with a start and sees that it's morning. And Miss Senia and Urania Mireta are up and busy making coffee, and Senia is singing aloud, singing at the top of her voice, delighted that the night is now past.

And candles and lamps have been extinguished, but out over the sea, the dogged morning sun sails and fights its way forward through wind and rain.

Afterword

As the title already suggests, this is no ordinary novel, but something at times rather in the nature of a dithyrambic prose poem. There are links back to Heinesen's earlier work, in particular the references to Ankersen, the sectarian leader, and the setting is clearly the Tórshavn of the early twentieth century. The novel's subtitle A Story from the Dawn of Time, however, already suggests a broader perspective, and this is indeed the essence of the work.

Heinesen's novels always contain the portrait of what might be termed a "good" woman: Simona in *Windswept* Dawn, Eliana in *The Lost Musicians*, Liva in *The Black Cauldron*. Here, however, the "good" woman, Antonia, is raised to mythological status as the representative of motherhood, the bearer of life as has existed from the dawn of time. This portrayal is placed against the description of a limited circle of ordinary and unprepossessing figures in a small town, much of it as experienced through the eyes of Antonia's infant son from his very earliest days until he is some five years of age.

In contrast to Antonia, who is portrayed in terms that recall the Biblical Virgin Mary, there is Trine the Eyes, an essentially tragic figure, whose tragedy to a large extent is the direct result of her narrow religious beliefs and her resultant refusal to follow her natural instincts and to take the chance of happiness and the natural fulfilment of life when it is offered to her. Religion, whether that of the official church or of the sectarian population, is in this novel portrayed exclusively in negative terms in stark contrast to the world of nature, the bearer of life, the supreme representative of which is Antonia.

The Black Cauldron – William Heinesen

"In *The Black Cauldron*, Heinesen provided an unsparing portrait of speculation, violence and intrigue in the Faeroes under British wartime occupation."
The Times

The Black Cauldron is not, however, a war novel properly speaking, but a work of magic realism which traces a serious of boisterous, tragic-comic events in one of the more unusual western European societies. Spanning the tragedy of war, the clash of sectarian interests, the interplay of religion and sex, *The Black Cauldron* develops into a presentation in mythical form of the conflict between life and death, good and evil.

"William Heinesen's novels are intensely Faeroese, but so universal in their appeal that the reader automatically surrenders to their charm, their energy, their easy intensity and is overwhelmed by the perspective they convey."
The Independent

£8.99 ISBN 978 0 946626 97 7 363p B. Format

The Good Hope - William Heinesen

First published in 1964 *The Good Hope* won The Nordic Prize for Literature. This is the first English translation of one of the greatest novels in the Danish language. *The Good Hope* is a masterpiece which took 40 years to write.

The Good Hope is a novel in epistolary form based on the life of the Reverend Lucas Debes, a larger than life character called Peder Børresen in the novel. In a manner typical of him, William Heinesen plays with both historical language and historical fact. It tells a story of brutal oppression, poverty and terrible diseases, but also of one man's courage and resistance to a tyrannical and despotic regime.

The Good Hope is a dramatic fantasy in which Heinesen's customary themes – the struggle against evil, sectarianism, superstition and oppression – emerge on a higher plane, set against the backcloth of the Faroe Islands in the 1690s.

£12.99 ISBN 978 1 903517 98 7 384p B. Format

The Lost Musicians – William Heinesen

"*The Lost Musicians* builds towards a crescendo of farce and tragedy in which nothing less than 'the cosmic struggle between life-asserting and life-denying forces' is played out."

Laurence Phelan in *The Independent on Sunday*

"Marooned in the north Atlantic between Iceland and Norway, the Faroe Isles are famous for little besides dried mutton and twice drawing with Scotland at football. Indeed, the thinly fictionalised island of this new translation by W. Glyn Jones of William Heinesen's 1950 novel often seems as much a prison as a homeland. The pursuit of happiness is hardly helped by the local Baptists, headed by tactless Ankersen, the spearhead of the prohibition movement. Set against his priggish faith are a colourful crew of musicians and layabouts: Sirius is a frustrated poet, the Crab King a mute dwarf, Ole Brandy a belligerent pillar of the community and Ura the Brink a cliff-dwelling fortune teller. One of their glorious but destructive drinking sessions is the stage for the novel's key incident, in which money is stolen and a young cellist blamed. The result is a tale of stereotypically northern European sensibility, in which merriment is bright, brief and viewed through the fug of booze, and desperation chips at the hardiest of souls. Heinesen's intriguing novel walks a fine line between a fable and a social document."

Jane Smart in *The Guardian*

£9.99 ISBN 978 1 903517 50 5 320p B. Format

Windswept Dawn – William Heinesen

Windswept Dawn is a Faeroese *Under Milk Wood* revealing the whole personality of a small closely knit community. William Heinesen brings to life a whole host of vivid, larger than life characters.

"One of the greatest Scandinavian novelists of the twentieth century, Heinesen (1900-1991) was a native of the Faroe Islands, in the North Atlantic halfway between Norway and Iceland. The Faroes, or, more precisely, Faroese life, are subject and plot, respectively, of this, his 1934 first novel, appearing finally in its first English translation. It would be more documentary than novel were it not for the keen psychological penetration of every character on whom Heinesen focuses in particular chapters and scenes. Among the principals are a Lutheran minister slipping into paranoiac delusions; a dour, suspicious, shrewd village shopkeeper; a woman innkeeper and majordomo-for-hire with a shrouded past; the philosophical and compassionate male teacher at a small island school; a bad penny of an evangelical Adventist missionary; a meek, compulsively eavesdropping, middle-aged itinerant; and a thoughtful, wondering youth just awakening to the world. The story, such as it is, consists of what these people and others think and how they interact within the span of roughly one year. Lacking all melodrama, it is the purest realistic fiction imaginable."   Ray Olson in *Booklist*

£12.99 ISBN 978 1 903517 78 9 504p B. Format